HARLEM AND HAVANA

A HOOD LOVE STORY

MZ. KB

Harlem and Havana: A Hood Love Story

WANT TO BE A PART OF THE GRAND PENZ FAMILY?

To submit your manuscript to Grand Penz Publications, please send the first three chapters and synopsis to grandpenzpublications@gmail.com

CONTEST RULES

THIS RELEASE WILL HAVE 1 CONTEST. THE CONTEST IS
REVIEW AND SCREENSHOT YOUR PURCHASE TO
contestsgrandpenz@gmail.com BY 1/17/22 TO WIN
1ST- $50 CASHAPP
2ND- $25 CASHAPP
3RD- $15 CASHAPP

CHAPTER 1

SIX YEARS AGO

I FINISHED SWEEPING the path and collecting the cuttings from where I had just mowed Mr. Roberts' lawn. He came outside to inspect it and once he was satisfied that I'd done a good job, he went into his pocket, pulled out a twenty-dollar bill, and handed it to me.

"Thanks son, you did a good job. Go up to the house now, Sally has a pie she made for you to take home to share with your brother and sister."

"Thank you, sir."

"Come back on Saturday and you can wash the car, too."

"Yes, sir. Thank you, sir, I appreciate you," I said as I walked to the front door, just in time to see Mrs. Robert's walking outside to see me.

"Here you go, my darling boy. I made you one of my delicious apple pies."

"Thank you, ma'am."

As I walked home, I was happy as hell. I had enough money to get some food to cook for the kids' dinner tonight, and even enough left over to get the things to make for them to have lunches at school tomorrow. I hated that it was my responsibility to make sure that Hallie and Harvey had everything that they needed. My mom was a complete waste of a human being. She cared more about her crack pipe than she did any of her kids. She left me caring for them ever since I could remember. She would disappear for days at a time, with no warning. There was never any food in the house, and it was up to me to do what I had to do to make sure the three of us could eat every day.

On the way home, I stopped by the store to buy the things that I would need and hurried home, so my brother and sister weren't left alone too long after arriving home from school.

When I got in, she was back. We hadn't seen her for three days, and then she just popped back up again and messed with the kids' minds. It's hard for them to keep seeing her like this and it's not fair on them, either. She was either getting high or bringing strange fucking men into the house around the kids just to get a fix. I actually preferred it when she did one of her disappearing acts, bringing up these kids was easier than putting up with the shit she did when she was here. We got by just well enough, but I knew I needed something more than just relying on odd jobs and handouts.

I'd watched this nigga named Slick, who my mama fucked with, and I saw how much money can be made selling bags to fiends. It was quick and easy money. I would be able to still go to school and look after the kids. I just needed to sell a couple of bags a day and we would be good. I wouldn't even need to be on the streets that long, so I knew I wouldn't get caught up with the police.

I made the kids their dinner and helped them do their homework. Then, I got them both to shower and get ready for bed before reading to them to help them sleep. They both loved it when I read to them, just to get lost in a make-believe world where everything was perfect for a while. I would get different books for them each week from the school library.

I could hear her in the other room. She was entertaining one of the many men that she let frequent our home and her cracked out pussy. I knew it wouldn't be long before they were high and in her room fucking, so I got on with my homework until I heard them leave the room. Usually, I would put my headphones in and drown out the noise that was about to start. She wasn't shy and didn't try to keep the noise down, so it was clear to anyone with ears that she was getting fucked again. It made me sick to my stomach, but at least tonight, it was only one man in there. There had been times when there would be two or three in there with her nasty ass.

I sneaked out into of my bedroom to get a drink. Walking past the family room, I noticed a leather jacket and bag on the chair. I knew then that it is was Slick in there with her. This could be my chance. I looked around to make sure I couldn't be seen and quietly I opened the bag. Inside there were hundreds of small rocks and a roll of notes. I peeled away a couple of the twenties, I stuffed my hand back in and pulled out a handful of the rocks. There was so much in there that I don't think he would even notice they were missing.

The next morning, I got up and got the kids ready extra early, hoping that we would be gone before they woke up. I told the kids to keep it quiet until we were outside, but just as they were getting their shoes on, Slick came walking out of the bedroom with just his underwear on.

"Yo kid, wait up," he called out to me. "Here, take this and get y'all some new clothes and some food up in here," he said as he pulled the roll of money out of his bag and handed me a huge chunk of it. "Don't let your mom know, she'll only try to smoke it," he added, before patting me on the shoulder and walking back into the bedroom with his bag and the crack pipe which was on the table. I felt guilty about taking his shit, but I needed it and I needed a way to earn.

I got outside and counted the money, there was over five hundred dollars. That was the most money I'd ever had in my hands at one time, and I was happy as hell. I hid the money in my sock and told the kids that I would take them for pancakes before school. They were so excited! They loved them some pancakes, but I usually had to make them because we could never afford to go out and get them at the diner.

After taking the kids to school, I went to an empty block where I'd seen loads of crackheads hanging around on plenty of occasions. I didn't have the first idea about how to approach someone and ask them if they wanted to buy drugs, but in the movies the guy usually just stood there and they came to him. I stood there for ten minutes before I spotted a crackhead walking up the sidewalk. Just like in the movies, he stopped and asked me if I was holding. I asked him what he wanted, and he said three, so I handed off three of the rocks and took the money. I stood in the same spot for three hours and sold all of the rocks that I'd taken from Slick this morning.

It was the easiest money I'd ever made, and from today alone I knew I would have to find someone to buy some from so I could carry on and sell more soon. I didn't know when Slick would next visit, so relying on seeing him again wasn't an option. Maybe I could just ask him. He knew my situation, so he might let me work for him.

I picked the kids up from school and took them shopping with the money that Slick had given me this morning. They were so excited to be getting new clothes for school, being that my mother had never took them shopping for clothes before. They had always had hand-me-downs from the neighbors' kids. The things that most kids took for granted, like clothes, food in the kitchen, electricity to turn on the lights, and a parent who loved you were alien to kids like us. I tried my hardest to be everything they needed, but at just fifteen, it was hard as hell for me. We had no other family, so it was no one who could help me. My pops disappeared a long time ago and never really bothered coming around anymore, so it was all on me to look out for the kids.

I let them get a few new outfits, and new sneakers each as well. They were going to look fly at school tomorrow. On the way home, we stopped by the grocery store and stocked up on some food before going into the pizza place and eating a whole large pizza by ourselves.

When we finally made it home, I was happy to see that she had gone again. I started putting the groceries away in the kitchen, while the kids put their new things away in their room. I pulled out the rest of the money that I had made and I was happy to see that I still had three hundred dollars left. I just had to find someone to buy some shit from now. I went into my room and opened my closet. Moving the boxes out of the bottom and pulling up the old, tattered bit of carpet, I lifted the floorboard and stuffed my money into the hole which I created to hide shit from my crackhead mother. When she was looking for her next hit, she would tear through the entire house, hoping to find some money or something to sell. I didn't know why she even bothered. Anything we had of any value was long gone.

After I put the kids to sleep, I got on and did my home-work. I was determined to graduate school and get us up out of here. Plus, if we didn't go to school then they would start asking questions. The last time we had to deal with children's services, they almost took us all away. It took me all day to clean up the house. My mother still looked a hot fucking mess but at least she stayed sober long enough to make sure we weren't taken. If we were gone, then she wouldn't get her food stamps and welfare. Each month, she sold the food stamps for crack and we were left with nothing each time. It's just as well that I had a plan on how to get us out of this mess. I just needed to find someone to get that work from.

The next morning, as we left the house, I noticed a car parked directly outside the crib. As soon as we started walking, the car started driving slowly behind us. When we were a few houses down, the car sped up and stopped on the corner.

A man that I recognized from around the way got out and started watching us. Instinctively, I pulled the kids behind me so they were safe.

"You Deanna's kid, ain't cha?" he called out to me.

"Erm, yeah. She's not here, though. I don't know where she is or when she will be back."

"Get in the car. I want to talk to you about something."

"I have to get these two to school. I'm in a rush. Sorry," I said ushering to both of the kids, and really not wanting to get in his car.

"Boy, I wasn't asking you. I was telling you," he said it with such authority I instinctively went to get into the car, but paused. "I'll drop you to the school after we speak. Get in, I just want to talk."

I got the kids situated in the back of the car and fastened their seatbelts before getting into the front seat. I told him what school they attended and he put it into his navigation system and turned the music up. The rest of the drive to drop the kids off was pretty quiet, he just said I was to drop the kids off and come straight back. I saw them into school and part of me wanted to run, but I was also interested in hearing what he had to say.

When I got into the car, he pulled off and started to speak. "What's your name, kid?"

"Harlem," I answered

"Harlem, huh?" he said with a smirk on his face. "Well Harlem, do you know who I am?"

"No, sir. I know that I've seen you at my house before, so I guess you be knowing my mama," I replied.

"Well young Harlem, I'm Big H and the block you were outside on yesterday is owned by me. When my boy got out there with his new product, the fiends were all high as fuck. They mentioned that a young boy had been outside with that ill shit earlier in the day and hooked them all up. After watching my cameras I saw it was you. Now, I'm going to ask you two questions and I want the truth to them both. Who gave you permission to sell on my block and who the fuck is you working for, son?"

"Erm. I. I. I'm sorry, sir. I'm not working for anyone, just trying to make a little something to get by. I found some rocks and I've seen enough people buying, selling, and smoking this shit my whole life that I knew what to do with it. The corner was empty, so I figured it would be ok. I didn't want to cause any problems. I just wanted to sell what I had and move on. That's all."

"And did you accomplish that goal?" he asked me.

"Yes, sir. I ran out completely within a few hours," I boasted, feeling proud of myself.

"Look, I've known your mom for a lot of years, so I know what she's like. It must be hard for you having to basically be the parent and looking after your siblings. I was just like you at your age. My mom ain't shit, even to this day. The block is no place for a kid like you. Look, I want to help you," he said, while pulling out some money from his pocket and handing it to me.

"With all due respect, sir, I want a job, not a handout. If I can work, then I can have a constant stream of money coming in. I appreciate the offer, though."

"I respect that, son. How about you take this and stop by my carwash tomorrow after school," he said, handing me the money. "You can wash a few cars after school each day and I'll pay you. There is one condition, though. You must go to school. You can bring the kids with you and they can sit in the office and do their homework while you work."

"Are you for real? Thank you, sir, I won't let you down." I was happy as hell. I wouldn't make as much as I would selling rocks, but until I found a way to get some more, it would do. Hopefully, if I proved myself to Big H and stacked my paper, I would be able to buy some work or even work on the block for him.

For the next few weeks, I picked the kids up from school, got them some snacks, and took them with me to the carwash. They would do homework or read while I washed cars. I wasn't stupid, and I could tell that there was more going on than I knew about, but I would soon come to learn the rules around here.

Big H dropped us off home one night after he finished up working and there was a man on the porch shouting at my mama. When we got closer, I thought I saw a ghost. This motherfucker could go right the fuck back where he came from. It was our bitch ass father. He left almost three years ago, and ain't been seen or heard from since. Big H told the kids to wait in the car while we walked up to the crib to see what was going on.

"Where the fuck is my kids, bitch? I told you already to make sure you keep them away from that nigga Harlem. Big H ain't shit, and you out of all people should know that, you dumb bitch," he screamed, only stopping when he noticed me and Big H standing behind him.

"Yo Marlo, my nigga! You gonna keep that same energy now we're face-to-face, motherfucker?" Big H said as he walked up on my pops, Marlo. I hadn't seen this nigga for years, so I was lost as to why he was saying that my mom had to keep the kids away from me. I was the damn reason his kids were alive with his ain't shit ass. He hadn't even called to check on us. He was just another unfit ass parent, just like my mother.

"Listen Big H, mind your business, man. Harlem, go and get my kids out of the car," he said turning to me.

"Motherfucker, you made it my business when you out here calling my name for everyone to hear."

The kids got out of the car and ran to our father. Being that they hadn't seen his ass for so long, I was surprised they even remembered him.

"I'm taking my kids until you sort yourself out, Deanna."

"Let me go get our stuff," I said, turning to go inside the house, finally happy that I wouldn't have to keep doing all this shit by my damn self.

"Na lil' nigga, I'm only taking my kids. You stay here with your daddy," he spat as he dragged the kids into the car and sped off down the street and out of sight, leaving me confused as hell.

CHAPTER 2
BIG H

I'D KNOWN Deanna since we were young. When we met, she was fifteen and I was seventeen. Back then, we were just kids with no responsibilities. She was the most beautiful girl in the world to me, perfect in every way. She was smart, kind, funny, and was already stacked in all the right places. We were always together. We were like best friends on some Bonnie and Clyde shit. After kicking it for a minute, we started doing what all kids in love do, and started fucking. We were young and at it like rabbits. We couldn't get enough of each other and fucked every chance we got. Everything was perfect between us, that was until I got a call saying that my grandma had passed away. We went away to Florida for a few weeks to help arrange and attend her funeral. My mama was already hooked on that shit by then, and I later found out that she only went back so that she could steal my grandma's jewelry to sell for crack money. After that, our family disowned her and she spiraled out of control.

When I got back three weeks later, I heard through the grapevine that Deanna had been partying and dabbling in coke, which turned out to be the start of her fall from grace. Not only was she getting high, but I was told that she had also been smashing a few of the homies. I was heartbroken, devastated, and I wanted to kill her all in one. Not only for cheating on me, but also for making me look dumb as hell out here in these streets. I was just starting to come up, I couldn't have my girl making me look dumb and acting like a whore. So, I cut her lose. Even at that young age, I knew better than to ever let the streets see me weak. A few weeks later she came back, telling me she was pregnant, and that the baby was mine. Of course, I was still angry and I didn't believe her, so I waved her off with some bullshit, and told her to come back when it was time for a DNA test.

A month or two later, she came back around with Marlo and he was claiming the baby was his. I figured that they'd gotten the test done and he was the father. She moved out of town after that and didn't come back until three years ago. After the shit with Deanna, I got my grind on and thought about nothing but my paper and these streets. My heart was broken after Deanna changed up on me the way she did, so I wasn't feeling getting into no relationships. I concentrated on making moves and stacking that paper. I only ever spent enough time with these chicks to bust a nut and keep it moving. Two years later, I met Vee and she changed a nigga's heart, for real. That's been my baby ever since, and she gave me the world when she had my seeds, so it was only right that I gave her my last name.

I'd always kept it a buck with Vee, so she's always known about Deanna, and it was actually her who had seen Harlem one day and made me think that he really was my kid. She snapped a picture of him and he looked so much like my son Brooklyn, I just had to find out if he was mine. The more time I spent with the kid, the more I actually started to believe that he was actually my seed. I'd been keeping an eye on him for the last few years, from a distance. Buying groceries, clothing, and shit like that for them, but never giving Deanna actual money. Harlem was starting to look more and more like my family by the day, so I knew I had to get close enough to find out the truth. That day I saw him on the block, I knew he had that hustler's heart and he was hungry for that paper, but the boy didn't have a clue what he was doing. If that had been one of the other blocks, he would've been jacked or picked up by the cops. That's when I knew I had to approach him that day. I'd planned on asking him outright but after seeing him struggle, I decided that it wasn't fair to just drop more shit on the poor kid. I decided to get to know him better first, so I offered him a job. If I could just get close enough, I could do a DNA test myself, and only tell him when I was sure. Part of me already knew the answer, though. The boy looked just like I did when I was younger.

Any fool could see that Deanna was too far gone for anyone to help her, so I knew I had to step in and help the kid out until I found out the truth about his paternity. What I didn't expect was that nigga Marlo to show up and blow shit up the way he did. But now I really had to step up and admit to the kid that there was a chance that I was his pops.

"Ma, what does he mean?" Lil' Harlem shouted at Deanna, snapping me out of my thoughts.

"Why don't you ask that nigga. Coming around here fucking shit up for me again, how am I going to get my welfare and food stamps now, nigga?" she said before walking back off into the house and closing the door behind her.

He turned to look at me. The hurt and confused look on his face pained me to see. I didn't want it to be like this, but I had to come clean

"There's a chance that I'm your dad, Harlem. I knew your mom years ago, but I never thought you were mine until I saw you recently. She came back around when she was six months pregnant, and from then on, she always told me that Marlo was your pops. Come on, you're coming with me tonight and we'll figure everything out in the morning. I'll answer any questions that you've got. Please, just get in the car. I took one of your soda cans from the carwash and sent it for DNA testing, so we'll know in the next few days if we related. But looking at you these last few weeks, I already know that you my seed."

He quietly followed me to the car, looking sad and defeated, which was never my intention. We drove back the house that I shared with my wife Vee and two kids, Brooklyn and Liberty. It would take about forty minutes to get out to where I lived, and I couldn't drive all the way there in silence, so I turned the music up and bobbed my head to the sounds of the tunes that played.

We stopped off at the mall to cop a few outfits, as he didn't have any of his things with him. Then we went into Walmart and grabbed any toiletries or other things that he would need.

When we got in, Vee was sitting at the breakfast bar on her laptop. When she noticed us, she smiled and stood up.

"You must be Harlem. It's so nice to meet you, I'm Vee," she said, extending her arms and hugging him.

"Hi, thank you for having me here tonight. It's nice to meet you too, ma'am," he said, shyly.

"You're very welcome, sweetheart. What a polite young man. I cooked for you both. H-baby, can you show Harlem to his room so he can wash up while I heat up the food."

I showed Lil' H up to the guest room, so he could put his bags down and freshen up, before making my way back downstairs.

"Baby, the results came in early. They were delivered this afternoon. I left them on the table for you. I'm going to serve your food, and then I'm going to head up and read to the kids before they go to sleep. I'll leave you both to speak in private. After what you told me about the way he was living, when those results say what I already know they'll say, I want him to move in here with his family. That baby needs love and support," she said before kissing me and walking back into the kitchen. I still wondered what I ever did to deserve this woman.

A few minutes later, Harlem walked down the stairs, having showered, and changed his clothes. He joined me at the table, just as Vee started bringing in the food. She had made a feast of steak, shrimp, mashed potatoes, collard greens, and garlic bread. The way Harlem ate that shit up, I could tell that it'd been a while since he had a real home cooked dinner like this. One thing about my wife was that she could throw it down in that kitchen, and the food she made was second to none. Vee was the kind of woman who loved feeding and taking care of her family, and I knew that she wouldn't treat Harlem any differently to how she treated our kids together.

"So, the DNA results came in early. You want me to open them?" I asked him.

"Yeah, ok," he said looking down at his hands.

"Boy, head up and chest the fuck out. Don't ever in your life look down like that. A real man makes eye contact at all times. You're a king and you need to remember that," I told him. Pulling the papers out of the envelope, I scrolled down the page to the bit that was important and started to read what it said. "Probability of Harlem Wright being the father of Harlem Latrell is 99.99%"

"Your name is Harlem? Shit, I guess you really are my pops then, man."

"I'm sorry I haven't been there for you. I was a kid when I met your mom, we were inseparable. We were very much in love, so I don't want you thinking it was just some jump-off. She was my first love. Anyway, I had to go out of town for a few weeks after my grandma died. When I came back, I found out that your mom had been taking cocaine with some people she knew. That changed her. She was out partying every night and doing things she had no business doing. Come to find out that she was sleeping with the homie Marlo while I was away attending the funeral of the best woman I had ever known. After that, I cut ties with both of them. I couldn't trust her anymore and I damn sure couldn't trust him. They were both snakes in my eyes, so I didn't fuck with either of them. Anyway, they left town for a while. When they came back, they told me that you were his baby and I believed them. I just hope you'll give me the chance to make up for it now. I might've missed the last fifteen years, but we've got so many more ahead of us."

"I'm down," was all he said.

"I want you to move in here with us. Don't worry about Marlo, just leave it with me and I'll find a way for you to see your brother and sister again. You know, you've got a brother and sister here, too. Brooklyn and Liberty, and I just know they'll be so happy to meet you. We'll stop by your mom's crib tomorrow when we finish work and get the rest of your things."

"Ok, thank you. But are you sure your wife won't mind? Like, she might not want me here."

"Of course, she'll want you here. You're my son!"

CHAPTER 3
HARLEM

BACK TO THE PRESENT DAY

AS I SAT in the jail cell, I couldn't help but think about all the bad choices that had led me to where I was right now. I'm sure life wasn't supposed to be this damn hard.

Ever since I was a boy, nothing was ever easy for me. I had to struggle for everything up until I was fifteen and I met my real father. After that, everything was easy, maybe a little too easy. I forgot what it was like to want more out of life, forgot the hunger which had always been my driving force.

Back when I was younger, I still had dreams and ambitions. That seemed like a lifetime ago now, though. I was still young and naïve back then. I was a humble brother who just wanted to make life better for me and my siblings. That was before I let my mind get taken over by money and power. Now, at just twenty-one, I felt like my life was cursed.

After going to live with my pops, I got settled into my new life with my new family. My little brother Brooklyn and Sister Liberty were cool and easy to get along with, but it made me miss my little sister and brother, Hallie and Harvey even more. Big H had been trying to get an address on Marlo, but no one seemed to know where the fuck he stays at. After checking with the school, we found out that he has pulled the kids out and moved them to a different school. Big H paid the school nurse to find the address for us. We drove out there to see them and Marlo made it clear that if we came back around, then he would make life difficult. This man basically told us he would call twelve if he saw either of us again. My pops said I had to take my time with this one, but soon enough they would be old enough and I could approach them myself.

After the first year of being in my new life, I had finally started to feel like this was my family. For the first time in my life, I actually felt like I belonged somewhere and had people that loved me caring for me. Vee acted more like a mom than my own ever had. It felt like my life before was just a bad dream. I used to see Deanna sometimes, but only when her ass was out trying to score. I tried to help her a few times, but she wasn't interested in anything other than smoking still. It pained me that she was so far gone that she had no interest in getting her family back, or even to have a relationship with any of us.

My pops and Vee tried to encourage me to follow my dreams and continue with school, but I had other ideas. Don't get me wrong, I'm clever as hell, but at the time I was more interested in money and bitches than continuing my education. Being the son of the biggest hustler on the Southside had me feeling like a celebrity overnight. People who had never looked twice at me were all of a sudden trying to be my friend, but I ain't trust not one single person out here. My newfound popularity had me feeling myself and I got involved in this gang shit, despite everyone trying to make me walk a different path. I was my father's son, so this shit was in my blood.

I was out in the streets heavy by this point and that's how I ended up meeting Mya. She used to hang on the block with her friends sometimes. She was a good girl in a bad neighborhood. She wasn't one of those ratchet ass chicks, she was a hard worker, but she used to play hard too. She was set for much bigger things than the streets and her parents hated our relationship. Their bougie asses thought she could do better than me, and they were most probably right. She had a scholarship to Harvard, had dreams of being a doctor. All of those dreams and hopes were shattered in the blink of an eye and the pull of a trigger. Just the thought of her could still bring a thug nigga like me to tears.

To the outside world, my life was picture perfect, 'cause I never let anyone see what was really going on behind the wall that I had put up. Apart from my pops and my right-hand man Kymani, no one knew shit about the real me. When I lost the love of my life to a stray bullet three years ago, I closed off my heart to the world. It was all about stacking that paper and hustling my ass off. I didn't have time for relationships. The only chicks I fucked with already knew the deal. They got the dick and maybe a little pocket change here and there, but that was it. None of that loving shit, no kisses, no laying in bed cuddling, and for sure no overnight stays. I would drop the dick off in them and leave.

The night Mya died, a part of me died, too. Shit ain't never been the same since.

We were at a cookout in the park with the whole hood. I was shooting dice with my pops and his crew when I heard tires screeching and the sound of shots being fired. I ran over to where Mya was, standing next to Mama Vee, to see her laid out on the floor with blood pouring out of her head. I couldn't let her go. I was praying for some sign of life. I sat on the ground, holding her and crying for what seemed like an eternity.

My father was trying to get me up so one of his men could drive her to the hospital. Eventually, Kymani pulled her off my lap and took her to the waiting car. I followed behind with my parents. Everything after that was a blur. I vaguely remember there being a fight in the hospital when Mya's parents showed up and they tried to have us all put out. They made no secret of the fact that they didn't want me dating their daughter. They thought she was too good for me, and they were probably right. But we were young and in love, so we didn't care. It was us against the world, and fuck who didn't like it. I knew in my heart that I would do whatever it took to make her happy and secure the bag so we could have a better future, a future that was now hanging in the balance.

"Get them out of here. It's their fault she's here. I never wanted her to date him. He's nothing but the son of a crackhead and a common thug. Now look at her! She's fighting for her life and all because of these people! God help me, please. How did this happen!!" her mother was screaming in the middle of the emergency room.

When the doctor came out hours later and told us all that Mya didn't make it out of surgery, my entire world came crashing down. I could hear her parents crying, I could hear people arguing, but all I could do was fall to the floor and cry like a baby. Mama Vee was the first one to my side, she sat right there on the floor with me and held me while I shed my tears. It didn't matter to her that we were in the middle of a packed emergency room, or that everyone around us was screaming and fighting. The only thing that mattered in that moment was her comforting me. That's just the kind of woman she was. Since meeting my pops Big H, Vee has been more of a mother to me than my own mother ever was. She's the best woman on this earth. That's my baby and can't anyone tell me different. I could only pray for God to send me a woman like her one day, but I don't think it's possible to get that kind of love coming around twice in your life.

The night Mya got shot, Big H put word out that he would pay two hundred g's for the person who brought him the shooter. We had everyone looking, but the streets stayed silent. It didn't matter how many people got hurt, not one single person had any information. To this day, we still don't know who fired that gun, but when I do find out it'll be a war and that's word.

For weeks, after losing Mya, I barely even ate and I didn't speak to anyone but my pops and Mama Vee. Ya boy was fucked up. When

I did finally get back to myself, I came back harder and stronger. I became a beast in the streets and took this shit to the next level. With the help Kymani and the crew, we were making more money now than ever.

Snapping myself back to reality, I heard the door to the cell opening and the guard calling my name.

"Latrell, get your shit together, you're getting out."

Two hours later, I was processed and stepping out of the jail. I had never been so happy to see Mama Vee in all my life.

"Hey baby, I'm so happy you're out of there," she said as she pulled me into a hug.

"Ma, I'm happy to be out of there! I'm hungry than a motherfucker. Can we stop off somewhere and eat?" I replied, while still holding onto her.

She knew I liked my food and those Bologna sandwiches they feed you were for the birds. I needed some real food in me. I didn't know how people survived on the shit they be feeding them in there.

"Of course we will, baby. But light this, 'cause I have something to tell you first," she said, as she handed me a blunt just as we drove away from the jail. "The night you got arrested, so did your father and some of the crew. Kymani got out this morning, the lawyer said they didn't have enough to keep you in, but it's not looking so good for your daddy. They've got wire taps on a lot of them. This is going to be a long fight and we need to get to the bottom of it. You can have tonight off, but on tomorrow, we'll have a meeting to discuss a plan. So make sure everyone is in attendance."

"Damn ma, shit is all the way fucked up. Try not to worry, pops will be fine. He's an OG, he can hold his own. We'll figure some shit out and he'll be home in no time," I reassured her.

"Boy, you don't need to tell me that. I won't stop until my man is by my side where he belongs. I don't want you to tell your brother or sister yet, though. I've told them both that he

20

had to go out of town on some business. I don't want us to have to tell them the truth. So, what do you want to eat?" she asked, flipping from one subject to the next without a breath.

"Anything is better than what I've been eating, so you chose."

I settled into my seat and put fire to the blunt. Picking up my phone, I dialed Kymani's number.

"Yo brother, what's happening?" I asked as soon as he answered.

"They let your ass out of there, then? I was starting to think they were gone keep our black asses locked down. We made it home just in time for the block party tonight, and I don't know about you, but I need a damn drink."

"I hear ya. I'm going to get some food with mama and then I'll hit you up," I said before ending the call.

Four hours later, I was heading out. I dressed in a simple black Balenciaga hoodie with matching jeans and sneakers. I grabbed the keys to my black Bugatti and made my way to the block. By the time I pulled up, it was packed out there. Cars lined the street and there were people everywhere.

I spotted Kymani posted up against his White Ford F150, talking to his chick Ashlee and a couple of her friends. As soon as he noticed me, he stepped away from them so we could speak. After chopping it up for a while, we went back to the party. That's when I spotted her through the crowd. She was the finest woman I had ever seen and I just knew that I needed to know more about her. Kymani must've noticed me staring, 'cause he nudged me just as the chick walked up and hugged Ashlee.

"Hey girl. You made it, then?" Ashlee said as she released her.

"Yeah boo, I told you I would," she replied.

"This is my man Kymani, and his friend Harlem," she introduced us.

"Hey y'all. Nice to finally meet you. Ashlee has told me a

lot about you both," the friend said sweetly, before they walked off together to get a drink.

Kymani turned to me with a grin on his face. "Yo, I told you that you Ashlee had some fine ass friends, bro. You know these pretty bitches flock together."

I just laughed. We went over to where the crew was sitting shooting dice and joined in the game. My mind was all over the place, but I couldn't help but keep trying to sneak a look at Ash's girl. I noticed that she wasn't paying any attention to any of the niggas who were trying to hit on her, which made me wonder if she had a man at home? I needed to find out more about her, so when we finished the dice game, I walked over to where they were both standing at the makeshift bar that had been set up.

After buying a round of drinks for us all, I handed Ashlee hers and Kymani's. Being the kind of girl Ash was, I knew full well that she would go and take it to straight her man, leaving me and her friend alone.

"I didn't catch your name lil' mama?" I said casually.

"That's because I didn't throw it," she replied cockily. "I'm only playing. It's Havana," she added with a smile that lit up her whole face.

"Well Miss Havana, it's nice to meet you. I'm Harlem. Why haven't I seen you around before?" I asked.

"I live outside of the city, so I don't come over here too much. Plus, I'm in school, so that gets most of my attention. But Ashlee has been asking me for weeks to come out tonight, so I couldn't let my girl down."

We spent the next two hours at the bar, talking and getting to know each other. She was so easy to talk to and the conversation just flowed. It was refreshing to have a conversation with a chick who wasn't all over me, or just wanted to be seen with the infamous Harlem. We spoke about all kinds of different shit, from school to family, and even what she wanted from her future, before Ashlee and Kymani came walking back over to where we were seated. At the same time, I noticed Shania pushing through the crowd with her ratchet ass friends and shook my head. I just knew it was about to be some bullshit. It's always that way with Shania, that's why I only ever fucked with her on the low. This girl always acted a fool, but she knew the deal.

"Oh ok, I see what it is nigga. So, this bitch the reason you can't answer your phone when I'm calling you then, huh, Harlem? Y'all got me fucked all the way up. Bitch you can move now, I want to talk to my man in private," Shania tried to shoo Havana away with a swipe of her hand.

"Shania man, don't come over here with all that ra-r..." I started but was cut off by Havana putting her hand up to my face to shhhh me.

"Bitch, the only bitch I see here is you. So, I suggest you move that ratchet ass shit out of my face before you really get yourself fucked all the way up. I don't play with basic ass bitches. I'm sure the reason he ain't picking up your calls is because you act ratchet as fuck and he only passes through to fuck when he's drunk. Just because a nigga give you the D, sweetie, that don't make him your man. Now, I suggest you turn around on your *Shoe Carnival* heels and walk the fuck away while you still can. I am not the one to play with. Trust me!" Havana shut that shit down with quickness.

Shania tried to swing on Havana but got herself punched in throat before she could even connect. Shania went down like a brick, and Havana stepped one foot over Shania's limp body and bent down to say something to her that I didn't quite hear, before fixing herself, swinging her hair and walking away with her hips swinging.

Everyone around us was laughing. Shania got up and ran off crying with her friends. Just as well she did, before I yoked that bitch up for that little stunt she just pulled. Shania was officially cut off from this point on.

I tried to go after Havana, but she got in her car and left

before I could even reach her. I was pissed that I didn't even get her number and I was even more pissed that Shania thought it was cool to act like that. Her ass knew what it was between us. She gave good head, but she would never be my girl. She was a ratchet bitch, but you know, them is the ones who suck a mean dick. All I knew was that I needed to get to know Havana better. The way she held herself was one thing, but that move she pulled on Shania back there had ya boy bricking up for real. She was the epitome of a bad bitch, and I knew I wanted her in the worst possible way.

"Nigga, I told you to stop fucking with that ratchet ass hoe Shania. I don't care if that bitch swallow yo' whole dick and yo' balls, she ain't nothing but trouble. Always has been and always will be," Kymani said, laughing as he approached me.

"Maan, shut the fuck up. You know I don't fuck with her like that for real. But hear this, where Ash at? She needs to get me that girl's number or something, bruh! Did you see how lil' mama handled herself? Mmmmph, that's wifey right there"

CHAPTER 4
HAVANA

I HATE for a bitch to bring me out of character, but I will not tolerate disrespect from these basic ass bitches. My daddy raised a queen and queens don't argue with basic hoes. Now, don't get me wrong, I will beat a bitch ass when I need to, but I don't like all that rowdy shit. I'm too pretty to fight and I pay too damn much to get my hair did to be out here like fighting like that. Not only that, but if my man or my daddy finds out about that shit, it would be just another reason that my ass can't come out of the house. They are both too damn overprotective of me, but for very different reasons.

My daddy is a big name in these streets so he's always kept me sheltered. Actually, so sheltered that none of my friends even know who the fuck my parents even are. He wanted me to make my own way in the world without being treated differently because of who he was. Plus, he never wanted anyone to be able to use me to get to him, so barely anyone even knew who I was. He kept his business and his family very far away from each other.

We have a great relationship. He calls me 'Heaven' and he said it's because I'm perfection, just like having his own little piece of heaven on earth. He's the best daddy a girl could ever ask for, but he don't play when it comes to me. If he even knew about my man, he would dead that shit without a doubt. He acts like I'm a baby still, but I'll be twenty soon and I'm planning to move out of the house once and for all. I know it's because he loves me, but damn, a bitch needed a break. I was sick of having to sneak away from the security and lie about my whereabouts all of the time. They needed to let me be grown and make my own mistakes.

That brings me to my man, Tip. At thirty-two he was much older than me, but I loved his ass and as my girl Aaliyah said, '*Age ain't nothing but a number*'. It's just a shame I was the only person who thought like that. My parents would kill me and Tip would for sure get fucked up by my daddy and my idiotic brothers. The only person who knew about him is Ashlee and she hated his ass. It's my own fault, 'cause I tell her too much about our relationship issues. Tip is a very jealous man, and he gets hella possessive over me. I would never cheat on him, but he always accuses me of shit that I don't be doing. But that's my baby and I know deep down that he really loves me.

Walking in the door to his house an hour later, I just knew this night would not end well for me. I'd already told my daddy that I would be staying with Ashlee tonight, so for once I could spend the whole night over here with Tip. I was already starting to wish I'd taken my hot ass home. Now usually, he's not in the house before it's almost morning. But tonight, he was sitting on the couch with a blunt hanging from his mouth, a half-empty bottle of Henny, and what I knew were lines of cocaine on a mirror on the table next to his Glock. Tip had the meanest scowl on his face. He stood up and staggered over to me.

"Where the fuck have you been Havana? And don't try lying to me, you little bitch," he spat angrily, as he grabbed me by my arm.

"Baby I told you, I was going out with Ashlee for a while to the party. Now, let go of my arm, you're hurting me."

"You were with Ashlee, huh? Well, this don't look like no damn Ashlee to me?" he said, as he thrust his phone in my face.

I saw that there was a picture of me at the bar talking to Harlem. Even I had to admit, it didn't look good. We were both laughing and he'd put his hand on my lower back. It had just been for a split second, but the photo had captured it.

"I was there with Ashlee, that's her man's friend. We were just getting a drink. They'd gone to dance and I didn't think it would be appropriate, so I went to the bar to get a drink and he came and sat down. It's not how it looks, Tip Baby. I figured it would be better talking to her man's friend than to be sitting on my own where anyone could try and hit on me. It was totally innocent, honestly baby. You know I would never do anything to disrespect you, I love you."

I leaned forward to kiss him, but he head-butted me straight in the nose. It hurt like hell. My whole face was instantly covered in blood. I pulled away from him and covered my face, and he shoved me to the floor. He started raining blow after blow to my body and my face. Each time I would try to get up, he would put me straight back down again. I tried to defend myself and started swinging back. I even managed to land a few hits, but I was no match for him. He was too strong and that shit he'd been sniffing made him even stronger, he was like the Incredible Hulk or something.

The beating went on for what seemed like forever before he started tiring. He stepped back to the table and went to sniff another line. I grabbed my bag, which had fallen next to me on the floor, and pulled out the Pink diamond encrusted nine that my daddy got me for my eighteenth birthday. Getting up off of the floor quietly, I aimed at him and fired without a second thought. I hit him in the shoulder and he went down. He went to grab his Glock off the table, so I fired again before running out of the door. I hopped in my car and sped off down the street.

I was so beat up, that I could barely see out of my eyes, they were so swollen. I told Siri to call Ash and waited for the phone to connect. I knew I couldn't go home looking like this, my daddy would see and demand answers that I wasn't ready to give, and there is no way I could hide out. Even in that big ass house, I felt like I didn't get a minute to myself. I prayed that my girl would answer the phone, but I was shit out of luck today. I tried to call her back several times, but still got no answer. I was so distracted that I didn't see the Bugatti pull out in front of me, and I went crashing straight into the back of it. Off all the fucking cars to hit, I hit the most expensive one on the road. Can you fucking believe my luck today? My daddy was going to flip the fuck out and probably kill my ass now.

The driver got out looking real mad, but hell, I would be too. He had his gun in his hand as he yanked my door open, and it was only then that I realized it was Harlem.

"Havana? What the fuck happened to your face, ma? I know you didn't hit my shit that hard."

"I'm so sorry, Harlem. I was trying to phone Ash and I was distracted. I'll pay for the damage, I promise. I need to go but take my number and call me so I can bring the money to you tomorrow."

"Fuck all that shit. I'm more worried about you than I am that car. Material shit can be replaced, baby. Who the hell did this to you? I saw you earlier, so I know you got hands. That tells me your nigga did this to you. Come on, you can't drive in this state. Park your car and let me take you where you're going."

I parked my car and got into Harlem's passenger seat. I had no idea where I was going to go, so I asked him if he could phone Kymani to get a hold of Ashlee for me. Calling out to Siri, he told her to ring Ky. There was no answer on his phone, either.

"They probably just fucking, don't worry. He'll ring back in a minute. Let's get you cleaned up and some food while we wait."

"I can't go anywhere looking like this, especially not in somewhere to eat," I replied.

"That's cool, ma. I know a spot," he said and winked at me.

Stopping at the drug store, he jumped out of the car. He came back out five minutes later with a whole bag of stuff to clean up my face. Turning on the interior light in the car, he started trying to clean my face up the best he could. He was so gentle with me, I couldn't help but look into his beautiful eyes as he cleaned my cuts and put a band-aid over the cut on my forehead. I took a couple of the painkillers he gave me and gulped down some of the water. I just knew that I would be in even more pain tomorrow.

I had to laugh when he pulled into the drive-thru. We ordered some burgers, fries, and sodas, and parked in a spot at the back of the parking lot.

I was starving, so I wasted no time starting to eat. Despite the amount of pain I was in, I managed to eat the entire meal. I always had been the kind of woman who liked my food but being with Tip I always had to watch what I ate. I wasn't fat when we met, but I was thick in all the right places. He wanted me to slim down a bit, so I did to keep him happy. Thinking about it, everything I did these days was to keep him happy. He had me doing all kinds of shit I had no business doing, and he was so demanding. He would tell me it was a part of being in an adult relationship, and the only man I should answer to was him, and not my daddy or my brothers. That was all well and good in his head, but he didn't know my daddy. I'd be answering to that man until one of us is in the grave and that's a fact.

We sat in silence for a minute, before he spoke.

"Why you letting that nigga hit on you, ma? You're too damn pretty for that shit. I bet it's not the first time, either. The first time ain't ever this bad," he remarked, snapping me out of my thoughts.

"It's the first time he's ever been like this. We fought before, but nothing like the way he was tonight. When I got there, he was mad about me being seen sitting at the bar talking to you. Someone sent him a picture of us together and he accused me of cheating on him. I need Ashlee to call me back. I have nowhere else to go. I still live at home, and if my daddy or my brothers see the state I'm in, then they will for sure fuck some shit up," I said, pulling out my phone and trying Ashlee again for tenth time, but there was still no answer. "I guess I'll just go to a hotel for the night. Would you mind dropping me off somewhere?"

"How about you come home with me until you get through to Ash? I'm not on no shady shit. I have a spare room and you're welcome to use it. But we can't sit out here all night."

"Thank you. I appreciate it," I replied, my gaze not meeting his. I was so ashamed that he had to see me like this, but he'd been so nice to me. I couldn't believe how tender he was when he was cleaning my face, and if it had been a different situation and I wasn't all kinds of fucked up, I definitely would've kissed those juicy lips of his.

Harlem is the first man I'd looked at since I met Tip. He was genuinely interested in what I had to say when we were talking earlier, and the conversation was so easy, it was like we had known each other forever. Now, because of Tip, he's always going to see me as a victim and it angers me so much 'cause I'm just not that girl. I was so scared to admit that I shot Tip, in case I got into trouble. I just didn't mention it. I can't get arrested. None of this was how my life should be and it had never been like this before. But everything was a mess right now.

CHAPTER 5
HARLEM

IF THERE IS one thing I hate, it's a man who thinks it's ok
to beat on a woman. The way Havana looked earlier tonight
was nothing like the girl that hit the back of my Bugatti.
Earlier, she looked beautiful, and when we spoke it was like
she didn't have a care in the world. She seemed to have such
a pure innocent heart. She was sweet and funny as hell. I
didn't get how someone could do that to the person they
claimed to love. She was beaten and broken down by that
man and I had every intention of finding out who the hell he
was and making his ass pay for what he done to her. But first,
I needed to see where her head really was at. The last thing I
needed was to bring heat and she go running back to him. If
that was one of my sisters, I would kill the motherfucker, so I
didn't know why she wouldn't tell her brothers. Now, I don't
usually believe in playing Captain Save-A-Hoe, but something about this chick was different. I didn't know what yet,
but I aimed to find out.

When we got back in the crib, I showed her where the
kitchen was, in case she wanted a snack or drink, and then I
led her to the guest room. I got her a towel and some clothes

to change into. I left her to shower and went into my bedroom and stripped down to my birthday suit. Turning the shower on and the heat of the water all the way up, I stood under the stream and let the water wash away the hundreds of thoughts running through my head.

I had to be up in less than five hours to go and see my pops and catch up with Mama to see what we needed to do. Big H always had enemies out here 'cause he was doing it big, but I could tell you, whoever had been talking to them boys about our operation would be wiped out with quickness.

As soon as I climbed out of the shower and put my towel around my waist, there was a tap at my bedroom door.

"Yo?" I called out.

"Hey, could we smoke something to help me sleep?" Havana came in, wearing my tank top like a dress with her hair up in a towel.

"Sure, climb up," I said, patting the space next to me on the bed.

I grabbed a blunt out of my drawer and put fire to the tip. Havana picked up the remote and put Netflix on. We sat in silence, just laughing at the TV, and passing the blunt back and forth. Everything seemed so easy with Havana. It didn't seem to matter if we were talking or silent like this, nothing felt forced. Glancing over at her laying on my bed, I just knew I could get used to this.

I closed my eyes for a second, and I was knocked out. The next thing I knew, I was being woken up by a banging on my front door. I looked over a saw that Havana was sleeping in the bed next to me. I pulled on some pants and went to see who the fuck was making all that noise at my crib. Pulling the front door open, I wasn't surprised to see Mama Vee outside looking mad as hell.

"Boy, you're late! And you know I don't like to be kept

waiting. You've got ten minutes to be ready to leave, and where the fuck is Ky? He should've been here by now, too. I can't trust you little niggas to get anywhere on time. Move out of my way, all standing there like you stuck on stupid. Go and get ready, Harlem," she was on form today. Usually, she was so placid and sweet, but when Hood Vee comes out it's a different story. That chick was always ready to cuss your ass out. But that's Mama and I loved that woman with all my heart.

When I got back upstairs, Havana had come out of my room and was looking scared. Her face was even more fucked up this morning and I really felt sorry for her. When she told me that this all escalated from someone taking a picture of me talking to her, it made me feel like shit. That nigga Tip was going to have to see me about that and when I find out what snitch sent him the picture, it was going to be lights out for them, too. I am too well-known in these parts, and regardless of this man's issues, everyone should've known not to violate and snap pictures of me on some shady ass shit.

"Don't worry, baby girl. It's just my crazy ass mama. I'm late for a meeting, so I got to go. There's food in the kitchen, so just make yourself at home. I'll be back later today. You're more than welcome to stay until you figure out your next move. Kymani will be here soon, so I'll tell him to get Ashlee to come over with some clothes and keep you company. Here, take this and go shopping to get everything you need," I handed her some money and pulled her in for a hug.

"Thank you, Harlem, you don't know how much I appreciate you," she said as she stood on her tiptoes and kissed my cheek just as Mama came up the stairs cussing again.

"Oh ok, I see what it is really is. So, you think you can stand your mama up over some pussy, little nigga? Oh, hold on!! You better not be the reason her face look so fucked up, or I'ma fuck you up personally! We ain't raise you like that, boy! What the fuck happened to her face?"

"Ma, it ain't even like that. We just friends. She got into a situation so I'm helping her out."

"Little girl, I don't know who the fuck did that to you, but you need to shoot that motherfucker in his ass and kick him to the curb. Ain't no man worth fucking up your pretty face for. Harlem, if you really want to help this girl, teach her how to shoot so she kill that motherfucker the next time he even raises an eyebrow in her direction."

"Yes ma'am," she replied sheepishly.

With that, I left there and walked down the stairs behind Mama Vee. That woman had no filter. I just hoped Havana didn't scare easily. Because if she did, then we would never work in the long run, and I had every intention of making her all mine.

Just as we got outside the crib, Kymani pulled up in his Benz and agreed to follow us to the warehouse for the meeting. I wanted to get in the car with him, but I knew better than that. After seeing Havana, I knew Mama Vee would want answers. I love her, but she's so damn nosy. That's my baby though, and can't no one tell me nothing about her.

Pulling up to the warehouse, there were cars parked all around the lot. She had made sure the entire team was here, from the heads to the dime boys.

I stopped to speak to Ky before going inside.

"Bruh, what the fuck happened to the back of your Buggi? You look like someone hit you in the ass, boy," Ky said as I walked over to him.

"Someone did hit me. You would know that if your drunken ass didn't pass out in the pussy again. I was so pissed, I walked straight over to that car ready to rip the head off the person who fucked up my shit, but it was Havana. Man, her whole face is fucked up from that nigga she with. He beat her ass so bad her eyes are damn near closed. You need to get Ash to go over to my crib and chill with her. She's gonna need clothes, so I left money for them to go shopping."

"She at the crib?" he replied.

"Yea, she's at the crib. Neither you nor Ash was answering and I couldn't just leave her. She's scared to go home with her face looking so fucked up."

"Ok. Ok. I see," he said while shaking his head with a huge grin on his face. I just knew he was laughing inside, but I didn't even care. This girl was something special and I could feel it.

Walking inside, I was shocked to see so many people. I knew our operation was big but seeing as we never had them all in the same room at the same time, even I couldn't believe the amount of people in attendance.

I went to take my pops' seat at the head of the table, but Mama Vee stepped in front of me and started speaking.

"Firstly, I want to thank you all for coming out this morning. I know you were expecting to see my husband, but sadly he is unable to attend. As you are all aware, I have spoken to all the bosses and shit has been shut down since Big H got arrested a few weeks back. He got pulled up on some bogus charges, but they're trying to dig up whatever they can find to make shit stick. I also have been digging around for information and I'm currently waiting for some of our contacts to get back to me. We should know more by the end of the day. Now, we need to step up our game. Someone has to have spoken to the police, as the lawyer was told that they had a witness who was willing to testify against Big H and the entire operation. Our job is to find out who it is and eliminate the threat to our livelihoods. I am going to need y'all to keep the shops closed just for a few more days. If anyone is short of money, then just come to me and I will help you. After all, we're family. I know it's a lot to ask, but I need us all to be on the same page. We can't afford for anything else to happen while I'm trying to get my man out of there."

I looked around to the room and noticed everyone's faces.

All of them looked to be with us but I would need to keep my eyes open until we worked out who the snakes were.

We walked out of the warehouse and made our way to the jail to visit my pops. I needed to see where his head was at with this one. Hopefully by now he would have an idea of who did this shit and how the fuck we fix it.

CHAPTER 6
BIG H

EVEN FROM THE INSIDE, I was the GOAT and I could still get shit done. I'd pulled some strings to get a family visit in the private visiting room, which was usually only used for lawyer visits. I was waiting for Vee and Lil' H to come in to discuss a few things which would help get my ass up out of here. I had also managed to find out the name of the person who helped put my ass here, and I needed to get word to my hitta to dead that shit ASAP. This motherfucker Yayo had been a pain in my ass for a long time, but he moved away and nobody heard from him in years. We used to be homies back in the day, so I'd always let him make it off the strength of that alone. But after this, he was finished.

From what I heard, he got stopped on some charges and sang like a fucking bird in that interview room. Luckily for me, one of the detectives on his case was on my payroll. The only problem was the other one had it in for me for real and was trying everything he could to get some shit to stick, which was why I needed to speak to my son and let him know exactly what I needed him to do. I already knew that without some action, I wouldn't see the outside of the jail for a very long time. I knew, without a doubt, that my son was a beast and he would do everything in his power to get me out of here. Despite only being in his life for the last six years, we have a bond like no other.

As soon as they walked in the room, I stood up to greet them. After kissing my wife and hugging my firstborn, we all sat around the table to talk.

"What have you found out?" Vee asked quietly.

"I've got a name. I need it to be dealt with properly so I can get out of here."

"Tell me, Pops. Let me deal with the problem," Lil' H said eagerly.

"It's Yayo. He used to be my homie back in the day, but he started acting funny so I cut him off a long time ago. It was a long time before I met Vee. He started acting real fucked up and was on some snake moves. I need the problem eliminated before he gets my ass locked down for life. I want to be the one to end that shit, but I need it done so I can get out. I want you to take Kymani with you and let him feel that heat, son. He's no lame, so you need to be careful."

"Yayo? Are you sure?" Vee asked.

"Of course, I'm sure. I wouldn't ask our son to do something if I wasn't a hundred on it. And Vee, I want you to sit down and not try to get involved. Yayo is not to be played with, as you well know. So, I don't want you doing or saying anything to put you in danger. We still have two other kids to think about. You need to make everything as normal as possible for them, but I don't want them going anywhere alone. H is old enough to deal with this without his mama thinking she needs to be there to hold his hand."

I noticed Vee went quiet after that. I sat and chopped it up with them for the rest of the hour before the guard came back and told me we had to vacate the room. Saying our goodbyes, I could see something wasn't right with my wife, but I couldn't address that shit right now. She always got in her feelings, which was why I never let her know too much about the street shit. I would phone her later and make shit right. But for now, I had shit to think about and she needed to be strong for the other two kids.

Going back to my cell, I pulled out my burner phone and sent my son a message with Yayo's address and the businesses where he could find him. I just had to sit back and pray that it wasn't too late. I couldn't stay in this place a minute longer than necessary, I needed to get back out and tie up some loose ends. Before I got pulled, I was in the process of making the arrangements for me to step down and let Lil' H take over the business. But until all threats to our organization were eliminated, I would have to remain in position. There's no way I would let my son deal with this shit alone, so it was imperative that shit was sorted before I made any moves.

Time went so slowly in this place, each hour felt like a day and each day felt like a week. I wasn't used to having anyone tell me what to do, so to be told when to get up and when to eat and when to shit, was doing my damn head in. You know a few of these guards were getting a kick out of seeing me locked in a cell, and it had them on some sort of power trip to fuck with real niggas like me, 'cause they knew they could never act like that in these streets. Don't get me wrong, some of them were cool for guards. But the rest of them motherfuckers were probably bullied in school to grow up with this kind of complex. The only good thing about it was that I got to share a cell with a cat I'd worked with for years. We chilled and played dominos for the rest of the night, before turning it in.

CHAPTER 7
VEE

MY HEART almost stopped beating when H told me that Yayo was responsible for him being locked down. My husband didn't know anything of my history with that man, and I swore I would take it to the grave with me. But I should've known that what's done in the dark will always come to light. I know I should've told him about my past, but I never thought I would need to. I knew I was going to have to come clean with Harlem 'cause he if found out that I had been lying to him for all these years, I feared that it would be the end of our relationship the way I knew it.

I met Yayo when I was fresh out of school, and that man was my everything. For two years, it was us against the world. He had me out here doing shit that I had no business doing, but the only thing that mattered to my young heart was pleasing that man. But that all changed when he up and disappeared on my ass.

I came home from shopping one day and he was nowhere to be seen. I tried calling him, but got no answer. I must've phoned him fifty times that night, but still got nothing. The first thing I did was clear everything illegal out of the house and hide all the money, thinking he had been caught by the police and that they would come to the house to search it. After two days of not hearing anything, I started to worry that he'd been in an accident, so I phoned around every hospital in the city asking if he'd been brought in, but nothing. I'd phoned him over and over again, hoping for some clue as to what had happened to him. After another few days, the phone had been completely disconnected. I felt stupid because, it was only then that I realized that I didn't know anything about him. I didn't know his friends or his family, and I had no idea of the places he used to frequent when he was out of the house.

I was as sick as a dog worrying about him, that I didn't even realize that I'd missed my period. I went to the Dr., and she confirmed my worst fear. I was three months pregnant and alone. I had no idea where the father of my baby had gone or if he would ever return. It's safe to say that I was at my lowest point.

I waited and waited for him to return, but he never did. I threw myself into work and trying to get everything ready for the baby. I found out that I was having a girl, and I was starting to get excited at the thought of meeting her. For months, I didn't know anything about where he went. Then one day, six months later, he came back like nothing had happened. I came home from work and he was sleeping in the bed we once shared. I was so pissed off at the nonchalance. How could he think it was ok to leave without a word and then reappear just when I was starting to get my life back on track? I went into the bathroom, got a jug of water, and threw it all over him. He jumped up looking confused until he saw me standing over him with my huge bump and the meanest scowl ever on my face. I didn't know what came over me, I just started hitting him and screaming at him.

He grabbed a hold of me and pulled me into his chest and I started crying like a baby. I had so many questions, but I wasn't ready to hear what he was about to tell me.

42

When he told me that his father had made him get married, my heart broke all over again. He had been in with this woman for four years and had two children with her that I knew absolutely nothing about. All along I was just a side piece and I didn't even know. I don't know how it happened. We lived together and spent every single day together, so I had no idea. I was totally heartbroken. I couldn't believe the man who claimed to love me had been lying the entire time we were together. The worst bit was that he actually expected me to stay with him. I couldn't believe that this man actually thought I was going to stay after finding out the truth. He really thought he could have us both still. I was having his baby, but that didn't seem to matter to him. He still wanted to stay with her and keep me and my baby his little secret. That's when I realized that the man I thought I knew didn't exist.

We spent the next few days together, him doing everything he could to get me to agree to his stupid plan. We both knew it was pointless. I wasn't the kind of woman who would knowingly be a side bitch. I told him that he would be able to see the baby whenever he wanted, but we wouldn't be together unless he left his wife.

I went into labor in the middle of the night. I must've phoned this motherfucker at least twenty times and got no answer. I went out into the street and hailed a taxi to take me to the hospital. By the time Yayo finally arrived at the hospital, almost five hours later, I was nine centimeters dilated and I could already feel her head trying to rip its way out of me. I was so angry at him. Just seeing his disheveled appearance, I knew that he'd been out with some bitch, and not at home with his wife when he got the call because he would've changed. That could only mean one thing, and that was there was yet another bitch. This nigga really didn't care anymore. He was really showing his ass. Between pushes, I was cursing his ass out for all to hear. I really didn't care anymore. I hated him with everything inside of me.

I'm going to take my baby and disappear. Yes, that's what I'll do... Ha. Who am I kidding? He'll find me wherever I go. I'm never going to escape this man unless I kill him.

I had so many thoughts running through my head, I didn't even realize what was going on around me. The nurse was shouting for the doctor to come in because there was a problem. When I finally snapped back into consciousness, I heard the nurse saying that they couldn't find the baby's heartbeat and that she was in distress. I was hysterical by this point and blaming Yayo. This was entirely his fault and I knew I would never forgive him. We were doing just fine until his ugly ass popped back up. One of the nurses came to my side, pushed something into my IV drip, and it all went black.

When I woke up, I was in a room with Yayo sitting in a chair next to the bed. I looked around for my baby but she wasn't there.

"Where is she?" I tried to speak but my mouth was too dry. He got up, poured me a glass of water, and handed it to me. I drank the entire glass like it was the last bit of water on earth and it tasted so good.

"Where is my baby?" I said, the words coming out clearer this time.

"I'm sorry ma, but the baby died during her birth. She got the cord wrapped around her neck. She didn't make it," he said, whilst trying to pull me into his chest.

"What do you mean she didn't make it? Of course, she did. She was perfectly fine and healthy. Get me by baby Yayo, and stop fucking around." I was shouting and hitting his chest.

"I'm sorry ma, she just wasn't strong enough," he replied, without an ounce of sadness in his eyes.

I don't remember much after that, I started screaming and

he called for the nurse to give me some sort of sedative. It made me sleep, but I could still hear what was being said. It was the strangest thing, but I enjoyed the feeling of euphoria, I could dream that I was with my baby girl. I could see her dark complexion and curly hair. She looked just how I had imagined her to look all of those months.

This asshole even had her cremated while I was under sedation. When I woke up there was a tiny gold urn on the table and a necklace with some ashes in it. He had the name Heaven engraved on the back and her date of birth.

I was eventually discharged from the hospital and he came to take me back home to the house he had bought for us. I went straight upstairs and as I walked past the nursery, I noticed that it was now empty, the crib and all the furniture gone. The Disney Princess mural and wallpaper I had picked out had been ripped down, and walls had been painted white. It was like he was trying to erase her from the house, like she never existed.

An hour later, he came walking into the bedroom.

"I'm going out of town for a few days. I have some business that needs my attention. I'll be back on Saturday. Will you be ok until then? Or do I need to get someone to stay with you?" he said.

"I'll be fine. Thank you," I replied without even looking at him.

The second he left the house, I picked up my phone and booked a flight and looked for an apartment. I waited an hour, just to make sure he hadn't forgotten something and wouldn't come back, before I started packing my things. I put all my bags in the trunk of the car and drove away without looking back. Thanks to Yayo, I had almost two hundred thousand dollars, which I'd hidden when he first disappeared. I went to New York and found an internship. I was there for six months before I met Harlem.

I forgot all about Yayo until Harlem told me that we had

to move back to Chicago. I just knew that he would cause problems if he saw me and that my perfect life with Harlem would be over before it really began. After living on eggshells for two months, I overheard Harlem and his friend talking about Yayo and the fact that he had moved his family to Atlanta and opened a club or some shit. I knew then that I could actually start to relax. I had no idea that they knew each other. But judging by the conversation I'd heard, they weren't exactly friends, either. I'd told Harlem all about my ex and everything he did to me. I just never told him it was Yayo.

I didn't think about Yayo again for a lot of years. Then around three or four years ago, I saw him while I was out at the bowling alley with the kids. He came walking up to my table and sat down as I watched Brooklyn and Liberty playing their game. He said he wanted me to pay back the money I had taken from the house, or he would make Harlem pay in other ways. I knew what he was getting at and agreed to get him some money.

I didn't tell him, but I actually hadn't spent hardly any of the money I'd taken from him, so it would be nothing to replace the little that I had spent from my savings without raising any suspicion. The only problem I had was the fact that I had kept all of this a secret from my husband for so long that I felt like couldn't tell him now. I agreed to meet Yayo and give him the money. When I went to meet him the following week, he counted the money and told me that he wanted an extra fifty grand on top of what I'd just given him. He started saying that he would shoot Harlem unless I paid up or gave him one more night of passion. I couldn't risk anything happening to my man, so I agreed to get him more money, 'cause there is no way that I would let that man touch me again. I loved my husband and could never let another man have what was his, even if he did have it first. That bruised his ego and he started threatening me. He then said that he changed his mind and didn't want money. I had one week to give myself up to him or he would hurt my family.

It was only when Yayo came and shot up the cookout that I knew I had to take matters into my own hands. It was his fault that Mya was dead and I knew that if my son found that out, then he would never forgive me. When we left the hospital, Big H went back on the streets to find out some information, so I left the kids sleeping and snuck out of the house dressed in all-black and ready for war. I drove to Yayo's house and shot at him when he got out of his car. I stood over him as he gasped for air, trying to breathe, and warned him that if he ever came near my family again then he wouldn't have to worry about Harlem, 'cause I would kill him. A part of me wanted to end him right where he lay, but I noticed a teenage girl who'd been sleeping in the back of the car. She was crying and screaming for her dad. She was about the same age as what my daughter would have been. I couldn't believe he'd just replaced her so easily with another child. I was livid; I fired another shot into his knee before walking away in tears.

He killed Mya and nothing would bring her back. I was so angry at myself. I spent weeks comforting Lil' H. He was heartbroken. He's never been the same since, and it's all my fault. Sometimes I fear that he will never love again. He turned so cold after losing Mya and I'd never known him to have anything close to a relationship since she died. That girl he was with this morning was the first female I'd seen in his house, outside of myself or his sister.

At this moment, all I knew was that I needed to get my man out of jail, and the only way to do it was to get rid of Yayo once and for all. I needed to formulate a plan to get him somewhere alone so we could talk. The only problem was that I didn't have a clue on how to find him. I would need to speak to my son and see what he knew without raising any suspicions. I also knew that I was going to have to confess everything to my husband, but I didn't want to tell him shit like that while he was locked down. I knew he would be mad, but even more so if I told him when it was impossible for him to react. If I were less of a woman, I would use the situation to my advantage and tell him when I knew he couldn't do anything. But I was cut from a different cloth. I would have this conversation when he was out, and then he can shout and scream at me all he wants. It's the least I deserve.

CHAPTER 8
KYMANI

WHEN MY TOP soldier phoned me and told me about the trap being hit this morning, I just knew today was going to be a fucked-up day. The place was back open less than twenty-four hours, and this shit happened. We already had enough on our plates with trying to find this cat Yayo, and Harlem wanting to kill Havana's man. It seemed like Yayo's ass had gone underground after snitching on Big H. This old nigga was nowhere to be found and neither was that nigga Tip. Now, with the trap getting hit it, was going to take all of our attention away from trying to get Boss Man free again.

I just knew that Harlem was going to flip out when I finally got through to him. Ever since the block party, he'd had Havana staying at the crib with him. Normally he would never let a bitch know where he laid his head, but he's claiming that she's different. I guess only time will tell. I was starting to think that my boy actually got a heart in that big ole chest of his. I hadn't seen him like this with a chick since Mya. They both claiming they're just friends and he told me that he ain't smashed yet, but it's only a matter of time before they got together. Any fool could see the chemistry between them.

Since Havana was there, I knocked on his front door instead of using my key, just in case I saw something that couldn't be unseen. Havana answered the door. Her face was healing and starting to look a lot better than it did a few days ago when I saw her.

"Hey Ky. I'm just cooking breakfast, you want some?" she said happily as she walked back toward the kitchen.

"Shit, can yo' ass even cook? Lemme see this food before I say yes to something that might well kill me," I laughed.

"Nah bruh, she can throw down. You know my ass wouldn't be eating nothing if it wasn't good," Harlem called from the breakfast bar, where he sat with food piled on his plate. I knew it had to be good, 'cause this nigga ain't like no chick cooking for him unless it's his mama.

"Yea, I'll have me some of that, too," I called to Havana.

We sat and ate the food before Havana left us to it and went about tidying up the kitchen. When I was sure that she couldn't hear what I had to say, I started telling Harlem what happened.

"Yo, the trap on 58th was hit this morning. Two of the little niggas got hit. They both made it and are with doc, so we can question them soon. Before you flip out, we ain't even lost much, just a couple hundred dollars, but no product. They ran out last night, and I had already sent someone to collect the bread. I couldn't get through to Tre to tell him to go and give them the re-up, and I was drunk so I couldn't do it. I told them to chill and I would be over first thing. But before I could get there, the place was hit. The clean-up crew is already over there fixing the mess. We need to check the footage from the cameras and see if anything pops up."

"I got the drop on that nigga we been searching for. He got a crib out in Lake View that no one knew about. I thought we could take a drive out there today, but we'll go by the trap first. "

We both said goodbye to Havana and left out of the house.

After stopping by the trap and checking the cameras we called a meeting with the rest of the crew. Someone knew something and we needed to get to the bottom of what was going on. I had never seen either of the niggas who hit the trap before, but I know someone had to know who the fuck they were.

By the time we made it out to Lake View, it was getting dark. I've got to admit, this nigga was living nice. The crib was huge and sat behind some big ass gates, and he had two men standing guard with AK's. That alone let us know it wasn't going to be easy to get to this motherfucker. We would definitely need a better plan. We posted up down the street from the address that Harlem was given. We waited an hour, before we saw a woman going inside the house, but there was still no sign of this Yayo cat. We hung around a bit longer to see if he turned up, but that motherfucker had gone ghost. Just as we were about to pull off, two cars turned into the driveway. We watched as two men got out, both too young to be who we were looking for. After watching them clowning around for a minute, I realized they were the same cats we saw on the cameras at the trap that got hit this morning.

"Well, ain't this some shit? They the same niggas from the fucking trap. That motherfucker Yayo had to have put them up to this. All three of them can get it for fucking with us, hating ass niggas. They living like they got that big bread, so this can't be about the money. This shit got to be personal and we need to find out what the fuck it is before we kill they asses," Harlem said.

"Straight. We need to find out what's behind this. He living better than any of us with his flash ass self," I added. "So, how you wanna do this, bro?"

"We'll sit on it for a minute. Let's get someone down here to watch the place and we'll come back when he shows his face. If he don't show by tomorrow, then them young bloods can get taken and that'll draw him out. He can't have gone too far or he just plain careless to leave his family behind," Harlem said, while picking up to phone to call one of the crew down to watch over the crib. We waited until he got there and then headed over to the strip club for an hour before it closed.

We went straight into the VIP area and ordered some drinks. Only the baddest bitches got to work this area. We had bitches flocked around us shaking their asses and titties in all directions, but all I could think of was Ashlee I wanted to get home so I could lay with her getting high and cracking some jokes. I've been out of the house so much recently; she hasn't really been getting the attention she deserves. Plus it's been a minute since I slid up in something warm.

CHAPTER 9
BIG H

I SAW the flash of fear in my wife's eye when I told her Yayo was responsible for this shit. She thinks I don't know that she was in a relationship with this fool all those years ago, but I've known that shit since before I got with her. Shit, if I'mma keep it one hundred, that was the reason I started talking to her in the first place. She told me about her ex and how he did her wrong, what an asshole he was, but she only referred to him as 'Fuckboy,' which always amused me. I didn't know it at the time, but Vee would become the love of my life.

Way back before we made it, when we were both just corner boys, we moved in the same circles. I would've classed him as a friend. His parents moved him out to the Eastside to try and get him away from the gang life, but that didn't work. He just got his own faction handed to him. What they didn't realize was that, even at that young age, we had earned our stripes. He carried on working, and eventually this mother-fucker used to run shit on his of the city. Everyone was happy and everyone was eating. As long as we all stayed to our own territory, everything was nice, but this greedy nigga wanted to take over and run the entire city. He fucked up when he tried to shoot up the block that we were posted on. He hit the kid of one of the older heads on the block and went into hiding for a while. I heard that he'd moved to the A, but it seems like he's back and had a score to settle.

I really thought that hearing his name again would make her tell me the truth, but she didn't, and at this stage it had me slightly questioning her loyalty. I'm hoping that it's because our son was sitting there, but we speak on the phone every day, so that's no excuse.

About six months ago, my day one, Smokes got out the pen after getting caught up on some charges. My nigga had been gone ten long years, and for something we all had a hand in. He rode that time like it was nothing and never snitched on any of us. So, when he came home, it was only right we looked out for him. I got Vee to plan the biggest party the city had ever seen. The whole crew met for dinner first, and each of us gave Smokes his homecoming gifts. By the end of the night, he had cribs, cars, jewelry, and more money than he'd ever seen. The party was dope, the whole hood came out to celebrate with us and we stayed up drinking and smoking until 6a.m., just like the old days.

On my way home, I stopped to pick up some breakfast for my wife and kids. That's when I saw him. Yayo was sitting the waffle house with a young girl, and they were just finishing their food. I walked past him to an empty table by the window. I heard him tell her to go and get in the car and wait for him. He paid the check and smirked as he walked to my table. I was cursing myself for leaving my strap in the car, I just knew by the look on his face he was about to try me.

"Harlem, long time no see, my nigga. How is your beautiful wife?"

"Don't speak on my wife, nigga. You ain't need to worry about Vee, I look after her better than ANY man she ever known," I said, smiling. I could tell straight away that my comment irritated his soul. The look on his face changed quickly.

"Smile while you can, but I'll have the last laugh," he said.

"Why wait, my nigga, let's do this shit here and now," I offered, but he walked away. "Na, I ain't think so, boi. You don't want them problems," I laughed as he walked out of the door.

I wasn't even fazed by this shit, I knew Yayo and he knew he couldn't do anything to me. This is what led me to end up sitting in this fucking cell. The only was he could take me out was to get the Feds to do it for him. They're the only crew in the city bigger than mine.

From what my source tells me, Yayo got held with a key of pure in the trunk of his car and fifty thousand dollars in a bag on the back seat. The second he got into that interview room, he started to sing. He offered up someone bigger than him to get a reduced charge. It's lucky for me that the detective was on my payroll or it might've been so much worse.

He managed to get a lot of what was said squashed due to the circumstances that led to the information being given. I still got pulled in over some bullshit, so I had to sit down for a minute while my lawyer did what I pay her ass to do. I was confident, though. I knew this would be dealt with and I would be home soon.

CHAPTER 10
HAVANA

THESE LAST FEW weeks things between me and Harlem had been great. We've talked about everything under the sun, and I just loved his sense of humor. He's so funny and smart, not to mention the finest man I've ever seen. I've never met anyone like him in my life. I've been staying here with him for almost a month now, and I wish I didn't have to leave. But I knew that I couldn't stay with Harlem forever, and my daddy was getting sick of excuses as to why he hadn't seen me. I knew it was time to take my ass home, but I was enjoying this time so much. Harlem was like a breath of fresh air to me. He was so easy to talk to, and we spent so much time laughing. It was a change to have someone around me who wasn't always on my ass. I felt like I had four daddies at this point – between my dad, my two brothers and Tip, I couldn't get a minute to fucking breathe without someone wanting to know where I was and what I was doing.

Tip had been blowing up my phone and leaving me crazy ass messages about how he was going to kill me when he saw me, and that when he found out who I was with in the picture he would kill them, too. I didn't know what I was going to do, but I also didn't want Harlem to get mixed up in the bullshit. I didn't want to take advantage of his kindness and I didn't want him to think I was one of these bum bitches who wanted him for what he had or what he could give me. I had my own, and I wanted to be able to see him again without it being awkward.

I only had the things he'd got Ashlee to bring me, so I didn't have a lot to pack. After I got my stuff together, I cleaned the house and then went into the kitchen and prepared him dinner for later. I made fried chicken with rice and mac-n-cheese, and a salad to go on the side.

I found some paper and a pen so I could write him a note.

Hey Harlem,

Thank you for everything! I didn't want to overstay my welcome, so I have gone home to face the music. You have been a breath of fresh air in the midst of the bullshit going on in my life. You have made me see that I am worth more than the bullshit I have been putting up with. I'm going to do what I need to do in regards to Tip and I will never settle for less than I deserve again.
I really hope to see you soon.
Your Havana.
P.S – I cooked for you, it's in the oven
Xx

As I stepped outside, I noticed that my car was in the driveway and it had been fixed. Harlem must've got it fixed. He knew I was worried to tell my daddy that I crashed.

Only then did it occur to me that I didn't have his number and I didn't leave him mine. I guess if he wanted it, it wouldn't be hard to get.

When I got home, my mother was the only person in the house apart from the staff. I said hello and went to walk up the stairs, but she called me back. I dreaded any kind of interaction with this woman. There was always just something about her. So much so, that I nicknamed her 'The Ice Queen'. All my life I felt like she just didn't like me. I don't know what it was. My daddy used to say she was jealous of me, 'cause when I came along, she was no longer the only woman in his heart. I never could understand how a woman could be jealous of her own child.

Anyway, I avoided spending any time with her unless we were all there as a family. It was only me she was like this with. She idolized my brothers. Neither of them could do anything wrong in her eyes. Even though I thought they were both idiots.

"Where have you been?" she said, looking at me intently.

"I've been with Ashlee. Daddy knew where I was," I replied.

"Hmmph. Well he is not here, he's gone off somewhere for a few days. No doubt with one of his whores. He thinks I don't know, but I always know," she said with such bitterness. "And your brothers are both out. I doubt they will be back any time soon, so I guess it's just me and you then – such fun."

I honestly didn't know why she stayed all these years if she really had proof he was cheating on her. I guess she was too comfortable in the life he provided for her. It afforded her to sit around in nothing but designer clothing, driving luxury cars, sipping champagne, living in this big ass house, while being waited on hand and foot. She really was a spoiled little bitch and I blamed my grandparents. They gave her everything she ever wanted growing up, so she expected my father to do the same. She hadn't worked a single day in her life. She doesn't even lift a perfectly manicured finger around the house. To this day, I don't even know if she can cook. I've never seen her in the kitchen unless it was to eat something the chef prepared.

"Um, ok. Well, I'll be upstairs in my room studying if you need me," I replied, unsure of what else to say to her.

Walking upstairs, I looked back and caught the way she looked at me with such contempt. When she saw that I was looking at her, she fixed her face to form a fake kind of half-smile.

I went into my room, opened my drawer, and pulled out a blunt. I opened the French doors to the balcony, went outside to my favorite spot, and sat down on the sofa. I lit the blunt and pulled out my phone to call Ashlee.

"Heyyy," I sung into the phone when she answered.

"You sound happy. Tell me you finally gave in and let that nigga Harlem get at that coochie," she replied

"Boy, bye! You know he doesn't want me like that. We're just friends."

"Ok, you keep telling yourself that. Anyway, what are you doing?" she asked.

"I just got back home. Did you know that he fixed my car? It was outside like new. When I got here, ain't no one here but The Ice Queen. I could've kept my ass there for a bit longer."

"Mmm Hmm, he's just my friend," she mocked. "Anyway, I'm coming over and we can do something. I can't leave you alone with The Ice Queen, she might try to drown you in the pool while your daddy ain't there," she said and we both laughed 'cause we knew it was a possibility with this mentally unhinged woman.

We said goodbye, and I sat back smoking my blunt while I waited for Ashlee to get here.

It was good to chill with my girl. We ordered some food and watched Netflix before Ky was ringing her to find out where she was. I walked her to the door and we said goodbye. I swore I could see someone standing across the road looking at the house, but when I looked back, they had gone.

I put the code into the alarm and activated it. Just as I got back up to my bedroom, my phone started ringing again. It was Tip calling for the hundredth time since I powered it back on a few hours ago. I didn't know what I was going to do about him, but I knew that I couldn't ignore him forever. Just as I was about to turn it back on silent, a number I didn't know flashed up on the screen. I was debating if I should answer or not, but then decided it might be important.

"Hello," I answered quietly.

"How you just gonna pack up your shit and leave a nigga without a word, ma?" the voice boomed down the phone.

"Who is this?" I asked.

"Who the hell does your ass think it is? How many other niggas you left today?"

"Harlem, I didn't leave you, boy. I just came home." I blushed when I finally realized it was him.

"My point exactly, you left me. You ain't in the crib where I left you this morning. Where you live at? I'm coming to scoop you up. I sleep better when you're there with me."

"I can't sleep at your house every damn night just so you can sleep better," I said, laughing at his silly ass.

"The hell you can't! You better not have gone back to that motherfucker who had you out here looking like Kung Fu Panda, with your Po looking ass."

"Good night, Harlem," I said, unimpressed by his comment. If it wasn't still so raw, I might've found it funny.

"I'm sorry, bad joke. Don't put the phone down, baby. Talk to me for a minute," he said, his voice suddenly sounding soft and sensual. "For real though, I've enjoyed having you here with me. I found your note and the food you cooked. You really know how to look after ya man, I appreciate that shit. I guess I was just getting used to coming home to you."

"Thank you for everything. You didn't need to do all that. You could've taken me to the hotel, but instead you took me to your home and took care of me. That shit goes beyond words. I just guess I didn't want you to think I overstayed my welcome. I don't want you to look at me as one of them bum bitches who was after what you could give her. Can I take you out to dinner to say thank you?" I said shyly.

"That is a first for me, ma. No woman but my mama, my sister, and my cleaning lady have seen where I lay my head. So trust me, if I thought for a second that you were that kind of woman, I wouldn't have let you in my home," he replied sincerely. "So, where are you taking me for dinner? You could just come here and let me eat you, I bet you taste sweet."

I couldn't help but blush at the last statement. He didn't know how much I wanted to feel him inside of me.

We made small talk for a while longer, before saying goodnight and agreeing to meet up the next day.

I went into the bathroom and turned on the shower. While I waited for the water to heat up, I put my playlist on and started singing along to some old school R&B while stripping out of my clothes. I don't know why but I've always loved this kind of music. Most of it was released way before I was even born, yet I would choose the old school over any of that new music they had out these days. It was like pouring your heart out through each song, and each song that I sang along to made me feel stronger.

After spending twenty minutes under the hot water I got out, dried myself, and applied my lotion. When I walked back into my bedroom, I almost had a heart attack. Laying there, in the middle of my bed, was Tip. His shoulder was still bandaged from where I shot him. He had a Gold Glock in his other hand, pointed in the direction of the bathroom. Without moving, he started speaking.

"Did you honestly think I was going to let you shoot me and live to tell the tale? I know you weren't with Ashlee all this time, so I'll ask you once and once only, where the fuck were you, Havana?" he said angrily.

"What are you doing in my house? If my daddy or brothers come back, they will kill us both," I said.

"Nobody is coming back Havana. Your dad is out of town

and both of your brothers are probably knee deep in pussy by this time of night."

"My mom is here, she will hear you," I said, wishing for one second I had a normal mom.

"Don't make me laugh, that old bitch will do what the fuck I tell her to," he said with a chuckle before shouting out to my mother. "Ameena, come in here."

I couldn't believe it when my mom walked in. She wasn't even shocked at this man in our house. He stood up and slapped my mom on her ass, before pulling her in for a kiss. The sight of it made me want to puke. When I get out of this, her days are numbered. Mother or not, she was a dead woman walking, and once my daddy found out, he would dig her up just to kill her all over again.

"Oh, don't stand there with your mouth open, Havana, it makes you look ugly," she said, laughing like it was a joke to her.

"Go and get daddy a drink, and let me have some alone time with Havana," he snapped his fingers, and like an obedient little puppy, she walked out of the room.

"Bitch, I'm gonna fuck you up for this! When I tell my daddy, he's gonna kill your old, sad ass," I screamed but this bitch didn't even turn around.

Walking towards me, Tip ripped the towel from around me and shoved me back onto the bed. He pushed my legs apart and hovered over my naked body. Putting one hand around my neck, he started to speak.

"Did you give my pussy away, Havana?"

"No, I swear I didn't," I replied, my mouth betraying me and not saying the words my brain really wanted to speak. I wanted to scream at him and ask him what the actual fuck he was doing. Why was my mom involved? And how did he think it was ok to fuck mother and daughter?

"You know, I will be able to tell. It will feel different if anyone else has touched it. This belongs to me," he said, roughly grabbing at my exposed, freshly waxed pussy.

Each time I denied doing anything, he hit me again. I tried reached for my phone to call for help, but he threw it out of my hand and onto the floor where I couldn't reach it, before I could press the call button. He grabbed both of my hands and tied them above my head with some rope that he must have tied there while I was showering.

"I swear Tip, I didn't do anything. Please just untie me and let me get dressed so we can talk about this," I pleaded, but it was pointless. He had already pulled his dick out and was trying to shove it inside of me.

I wrestled to get free. I was begging him to stop, but he didn't. It's like he was possessed, he just kept fucking me and it hurt.

"You shot me, you bitch!" he said angrily as he thrust in and out of me with no mercy.

He kept thrusting in and out of me. The entire time he was talking shit about how he owned me and that he knew I had been fucking someone else. Each time I cried, he hit me in my face. But each time he hit me it made me cry out again. Blow after blow, he just kept hitting me and hitting me until it all went black.

CHAPTER 11
TIP

I COULDN'T BELIEVE it when I first got that picture of Havana sitting at the bar talking to this little nigga. I didn't know who the fuck he was, but from what I heard, he was a big name in these streets. I didn't care how big he was, though. He wouldn't touch what was mine and think it was ok. He needed to be taught a lesson, and so did Havana. That's the problem with kids these days, they had no damn respect.

I put the word out there that I wanted the drop on this motherfucking Harlem, but no one was biting. The trick that sent me the picture was just some little thot from the projects that I fucked with from time-to-time. She's more than a little salty about my relationship with Havana. Mainly because of her age, but also because she was my main side bitch before Havana came into the picture. But now I only saw her from time-to-time. Now, I know she only sent the picture to be messy, but I didn't care. I needed eyes and ears out on the streets, and she was happy to give me all the information that she'd heard, and she got very well compensated for her efforts. Usually with dick, but I also threw her some change every now and then to keep her sweet.

The more I drank, the angrier I became. I knew I shouldn't have started sniffing those lines, but I couldn't help myself. The more waved I got, the more I thought of how much I was going to fuck up Havana and then go after this little nigga Harlem. I just kept staring at the picture and I got madder and madder. Shit, I might just make her help me set him up. She would be my way to get to him.

By the time she walked in the door I was too far gone. Normally, I would never dream of hitting her face, but that night I lost my shit and her smart ass mouth didn't help the situation. She was trying to play me like I was stupid. I lost my mind and just kept hitting her like she was a nigga on the street.

Never in a million years did I expect what happened next. I'd never seen her with a gun before, and she played so innocent, so I never imagined she would actually be strapped. When this bitch fired at my shoulder, I went down like a brick. I reached for my strap and she fired again, this time it missed me by inches and hit the table. Before I could even gather my thoughts, this bitch was gone. She didn't even flinch when she shot me, which told me this bitch had fired a gun more than once.

I was under pressure from this bitch Ameena. She's constantly in my ear about one thing or another. It was her idea for me to get close to Havana. She wanted me to pretend to be her boyfriend and get her hooked on drugs. When she was hooked, I would overdose her and she would die. Then her husband would break down and we could take everything from under him. Now she just wanted me to kill her husband and Havana so we could be together.

I only ever got involved in this for the money. I didn't want either of them, really. I was all for the plan originally, but when I saw Havana's little virgin ass, I just had to have her. But now they were both too high maintenance for my liking. I'd be damned if I walked away now, though. I'd put in too much time and put up with too much shit to walk away without getting paid.

This little bitch had been ghost for two whole weeks after shooting me. So when Ameena phoned and told me that she had come home, I knew it was my chance to get her. I had been at her house every night for the last week, since Ameena's husband went out of town. Her clown ass sons were nothing for me to worry about. I could take both of them out in a heartbeat.

I parked my car across the street and finished smoking my blunt, when I saw Ashlee pull up on the driveway of their house. Fucking typical, this little bitch was always in my way. She never made a secret of the fact she hated me being with Havana, it was probably her idea to try and set her up with this little nigga Harlem. It seemed like hours I was left outside waiting for her to leave. I got comfortable and pulled out a little bag of white powder and made a line on the back of my phone. One line turned into five and I was high as fuck. When I finally saw the door open and Ashlee drive off, I prepared myself for what I was about to do.

Ameena let me in the front door, standing there in nothing but a robe, which she'd purposely left open so I could see her body. I had to admit, she was stacked in all the right places and beautiful for a woman of her age. She had the perfect hour-glass figure with a fat ass, but it was clearly sculpted and paid for by her rich husband. Havana, on the other hand, she was naturally stacked and had the perfect body. It made it more perfect that it had only been touched by me. Just the thought of it was making me hard. I knew she would put up a fight but I didn't care. She was about to learn who the fuck daddy was up in this bitch now.

Before the front door was even closed properly, Ameena was on her knees swallowing my dick whole. Grabbing at her hair, I guided her head up and down while thinking about Havana's tight little box. The way she was slurping and moaning sent me over the edge and within minutes, I was shooting my seeds down her throat. Like the pro she was, she didn't miss a drop. I could see the wet patch in her panties. She was ready for me to fuck her right there where we stood. She pulled me over to the bottom of the huge winding staircase and bent over, spreading her cheeks. Due to the amount of coke I had sniffed, I was horny as fuck and hard again already. She was screaming so loud while I gave her them death strokes, I had to tell her to shut up before Havana heard us.

When I'd finished, I put my junk away and walked up the stairs to find Havana. I knew exactly where her room was because what nobody knew, was that I came here all the time when Ameena was home alone. But this was the first time I had used the front door as there were usually guards walking around out there.

I walked into her room quietly and closed the door behind me. I could hear her from the shower singing those sad ass old tunes that she loved so much. I made myself comfortable and waited for her.

When she walked in, I could tell she was scared to see me there. She actually thought calling for her mama would help. When I touched her, I knew she had given away what was supposed to be mine. I had to make her pay for what she did to me. The pain in my arm was a constant reminder of the betrayal. I took off my belt and beat her ass like a kid that stole something, until I was out of breath. I didn't mean to hurt her so bad, but she just got me so mad. I tell you this bitch made me lose my damn mind. I didn't care anyway; I was going to get what I could now and then disappear.

CHAPTER 12
HARLEM

THE LAST FEW weeks with Havana had been amazing. I never thought I would ever feel anything like this for a chick again. Each night when I get home from running the streets, she was there, looking more and more beautiful, with a home cooked meal waiting on me. After we ate, we'd usually go and chill on my bed and smoke while watching movies. It was all so effortless with her, and the more I got to know her, the more I was certain that she was going to be mine. The only thing was that we still hadn't fucked. I made her cum a few times when we were fooling around, but I couldn't give her the dick until I was certain that she was ready. Once I dropped this dick off in her, it was a wrap. She was wifey for lifey and she ain't even realize it yet.

I couldn't believe it when I got home tonight and Havana wasn't here. I should've been happy to have my space back, but I was getting used to having her here. I'm not gonna front, I'm feeling lil' mama something bad. I pulled out my phone to call Ky.

"Yo, send me Havana's number, bruh. I just got back and she gone ghost on ya boy," I said into the phone.

All this dumb motherfucker did was laugh at my ass. I ended the call, and went into the kitchen.

I was shocked to see a note from her, thanking me and letting me know she cooked for me.

As I was heating up the food, my phone pinged with a message from Kymani. I opened the message and it was just a number with a load of laughing emojis. You know, the ones with the tears flying out. I just responded with one big black middle finger emoji.

I just knew he was getting a kick out of this. It had been years since I was really feeling a chick and he knew it. All those damn laughing faces on my screen was irritating as hell. It's all love, though. That's my day one. If anyone else jumped out of pocket like that, it might be a problem.

I grabbed my food, put a bit of hot sauce on it, and sat at the breakfast bar. I pressed the number in the message and waited for an answer. I was just about to disconnect the call when she answered.

We spoke for the next forty minutes. She was so easy to speak to and she made me laugh so much, something that not many chicks could do. We agreed to meet the next day as she wanted to go out for dinner to say thank you. I would never let her pay, but it was a good enough excuse to see her again, so I agreed.

About an hour later, I was in bed and I heard my phone vibrating on the side. I got up to answer it and saw Havana's name on the screen.

I answered it, but she wasn't responding. I thought she must've pocket dialed me. I listened for a second longer and heard a man's voice. Instantly, my blood started boiling at the thought of her with another man. Then I could hear her crying, begging him to stop. I could hear him hitting her, and her crying out in pain.

I pulled out my hoe phone and dialed Ky's number, never disconnecting from Havana's call. My hoe phone was a phone solely used for hoes. I couldn't have these crazy bitches on my actual line, now could I?

"Ky, get me Havana's address. She pocket dialed me and I can hear someone fucking some shit up in the background. We need to go and make sure she ok. Where is Ash?" I said, without taking a breath. I didn't have time for shit. I needed to get to Havana quickly.

Five minutes later, I heard tires screeching outside, as Ky pulled up with a crying Ashlee in the car.

I gave the phone to Ashlee so she could listen and tell me if she recognized the man's voice.

"It's Tip," she answered between sobs.

"Tell me everything you know about this nigga, Ash."

She started telling us how this nasty motherfucker was thirty damn two years old and lived over by Cicero. I sent a text to my PI to find me any information he could on this cat. Something was telling me that I needed to know who this motherfucker was.

I wasn't even paying attention to where Ashlee was driving to until she pulled into this big ass driveway. I looked up and realized that this was the same address in Lake View as what we had for this Yayo motherfucker.

"What the fuck is going on?" Kymani shouted, as his Glock pointed straight at Ashlee's head.

"Yo, is this some sort of fucking game, Ash? You tryna set us up?" I demanded, pulling my .40 out and aiming it at her quickly. I couldn't believe this bitch was trying to set us up.

"You told me to bring you to Havana. This is her house." she said, visibly scared. "I don't know what is going on, but take them damn guns out of my fucking face. We need to get in there and get to her. I don't know what the fuck is wrong with you two sometimes, but I'm done with both your crazy asses after this."

"Lead the way, then," Kymani said, not lowering his gun and not taking his eyes off her. I knew exactly what he was doing, and if this was a set up, then she would get hit first. I knew this was difficult for him, he didn't know if his woman could be trusted. But I was happy to see that he was still thinking with his head and not his dick.

We didn't see a single person in the house, which I thought was strange, because last time I came here there were motherfuckers walking around outside with AK's. I wondered to myself where they were now. All I knew was that if this was some sort of fuckery shit, then it wouldn't end well for Ash or Havana.

We got up to Havana's room and she was laying naked on the bed with blood pouring from her face and cuts all over her body. I pushed past the others. In that second I didn't think about anything, I just ran to her. Seeing her so helpless took my mind back to when Mya was shot. I think Kymani noticed it, 'cause he came up behind me and covered her body with the towel that was near her while checking for a pulse.

Ashlee was screaming hysterically by this stage and we still didn't know if anyone was still in the house.

"Ash, take my gun and aim it at the door. If anyone walks in, shoot them. Don't think twice, do you hear me?" Kymani shouted to her, and she just nodded her head and took the gun from his hand.

We took Havana into the bathroom and put her under the water. She woke up quickly and with the most scared expression ever on her face. It pained me to see her hurt again. I knew I had to kill this motherfucker and I was so angry with myself because I knew I should've done it the first time he put his hands on her.

When she saw it was me holding her, she burst into tears. Grabbing me tight, she held on to me and cried.

"Harlem, you came. You saved me again. I love you," she said, before passing out.

"Come on baby, stay with me. It's going to be ok. Just

open your eyes. I love you too, ma, just stay with me," I said, tears falling from my own eyes. "We need to get her to the hospital. This can't happen again. I won't let this happen again. Come on, let's go."

"She's gonna be fine, Harlem. This isn't Mya. You need to calm down. I need you to stay focused, 'cause you can't lose it yet, bruh. Come on, let's get her to the car. Ashlee, you need to take her to the hospital now. Don't stop for anything, ok, baby girl? We need to search this place and see where this motherfucker got to." Kymani was taking charge and right now, that was exactly what I needed him to do.

My mind was somewhere else. Just looking at her beautiful face, I couldn't believe that someone could do this to her. I needed to find this Tip character and kill him for what he had done to her. The feeling of Kymani taking her from my arms and laying her on the back seat of the car snapped me out of the trance I was in.

As I spoke, I kissed the top of Havana's head. "I'mma be right behind you, baby. Just wait for me, ok. Don't close your eyes, Havana. You hear me ma? Ash, make sure she keeps talking. Please Ash, just get her there."

Closing the door, Ashlee sped off to the hospital.

"You know we need to get in here and get a look around. We need to find out how she is connected to this cat Yayo and them little joker ass motherfuckers who robbed an empty trap and hit the youngsters," Kymani said as he pulled out his phone and shot a text over to Dre, telling him to come scoop us up.

We walked back inside the house and started to look around. It was empty. Not a soul in sight. We went into each of the rooms, looking around as we went. We walked back upstairs, and that's when I heard a noise coming from one of the bedrooms.

I nodded to Ky and we both walked to the door. Opening the door, I could see two people in the bed fucking. *What the hell is going on? They must've heard her crying, or did they just not care?*

I let off a shot in the man's ass and as soon as he jumped up, I shot the woman in the foot. We grabbed them both and tied them up with their own clothes.

"Who are you and what are you doing in my house? You idiots, do you even know who my husband is? He will kill you for this!" the woman started shouting.

Judging by the look on the man's face, this was not her husband.

"Ah look, it's Captain Save-A-Hoe and his little sidekick," the man spat.

"Ain't shit little about me motherfucker. Just ask yo' mama," Kymani said, laughing at his own joke.

"You ain't shit motherfucker. You both just little boys playing a big man's game. Just untie me and we can talk about it."

"Well ain't that something! I heard Havana crying the same thing before you beat her and raped her."

"I didn't rape her, she was begging for it," he laughed, as if he was taunting me. I don't know what came over me; I punched him straight in the mouth. I hit him so damn hard he almost fell back in the chair. He smirked at me, so I pulled my .40 and shot him straight in the head. I was sick of the shit he was talking, and now he would never be able to talk shit again. I fired off one more shot in his chest just for good measure. The woman, who was in the splash zone, was now covered in her lover's blood and screaming like a hungry baby wanting to be fed.

"Damn nigga, you could've warned me. I would've moved so I didn't end up with this brain splatted all over my damn shoes. I told you before about that shit, man. What are we gonna do with her now?" Ky asked me, motioning to the screaming woman tied up in front of us.

"We're taking her with us. We can use her as bait to draw

this slimy cat out of his hole," I said, like the answer was obvious.

"My husband will find you and kill you both, and if he doesn't, my sons will. You stupid little boys, you don't know what you've started. There will be a war in the streets behind me, just you wait and see. You will pay for this! How could you kill him like he was nothing? You make me sick. When I get out of this, I swear to God I'll make you pay," the woman was ranting on.

"Bitch, shut the fuck up. You're more worried about your side nigga than your own daughter! Where the fuck they do that at, bruh? I'm gonna make you pay for what he did to Havana. How could you be in here fucking that man knowing what he'd just done to her? To your own daughter? You're one sick motherfucker. You can't do shit, and when I get your husband and dumb ass sons, they're gonna meet the same fate as him. I'm going to leave you alive until last, so you can see me destroy everything close to you. Snake ass hoe," I shouted back.

"That little bitch makes me sick! I wish he had never brought her home to me. I tried to get rid of her more than once, but it never worked. She's not my fucking daughter. My husband gave me her to make up for the fact that I couldn't have more children after my youngest son was born. I had a complicated labor due to not being able to get to the hospital quick enough, while my husband was out fucking that whore Valencia. When they told me I couldn't have any more children I was heartbroken because I had always wanted a daughter, but not her! She makes me sick, and every day it's a constant reminder that my husband had some other bitch pregnant with his child." Each word was spat with so much venom, I could feel the hatred she had for Havana and it made my blood boil.

"Help me put something on this old bitch. I don't wanna see them saggy ass titties no more," Ky laughed. He always tried to lighten the mood, but he was the one person I knew that always had my back.

"Let's do this and get the fuck out of here. I need to get to the hospital."

We dragged this bitch kicking and screaming outside to where Dre was waiting in the Benz, arguing with this chick on the phone. After putting her in the trunk, I told Dre to get me to the hospital. Kymani phoned Ashlee to find out what was happening.

"Yo, who is the bitch and why the fuck is she in the trunk?" Dre finally spoke.

"It's a long story. Just take her to the warehouse and keep her tied up. I want her alive when I get there."

Dre just nodded his head and drove us to the hospital.

When we got in there, we went straight to her room. She looked so helpless laying here in the bed. Ashlee said they had given her something to sedate her to help with the pain. She had internal bleeding from the beating that he gave her and cuts all over her body, but she would be fine.

I sat down next to her and held her hand. In this moment, I was torn. I needed answers, but I needed her to be ok. I just couldn't get my head around any of this. I had this woman in my crib. If she was on some set up type shit, then she was damn good at it. This was what happened when niggas think with their dicks, not their minds. I knew I should've dropped her at the hotel and kept it pushing.

"Yo Ash, what do you know about her family?" I asked.

"Erm, well she lives at home with her mom, dad and two brothers. She doesn't get on with her mom, she never has. The woman gives off some weird vibes. She's daddy's little princess. I think her dad is in the streets heavy. I mean, just look at the house she lives in, and that's not the only house they have. I've only ever seen him a few times. He always kept her sheltered from that side of his life. Her brothers are older, but they both still live at home. I don't really know them, but from what she says, they're on her ass just as much as her dad is. Just because I told you all that, it doesn't mean I forgive either of your funky asses for holding guns in my face."

"Oh yea, about that..." I started but was cut off by Kymani.

"Nah, fuck all that. We ain't sorry about that. We thought you were trying to set us up. I'm not sorry. Ashlee, you have to understand the life we're in, and if I thought you were on some fuckery shit, I would shoot you in the pussy and not think twice," he said.

Ashlee stood up and walked out of the room without a word, but if looks could kill, we would be two dead mother-fuckers up in here.

"Bruh, how you gonna threaten to shoot her in the pussy? You know you better go find her ass before you ain't see no pussy 'til Christmas," I managed to get out between laughing. This motherfucker was always with this shit.

Kymani got up and followed Ash, leaving me in the room with Havana.

"I don't know what it is about you girl, but if you end up being a snake, I might just shoot you in your pussy, too," I said, even though I knew she couldn't hear me. I held onto her hand just a little bit longer, before I got up to leave.

Just as I made it to the door of the room she was staying in, Ashlee came back with Ky.

"Her dad is on the way here, he just returned my calls," Ash said.

"Keep me updated, Ash. Let me know the second her eyes are open," I said before turning to Kymani. "You ready to get out of here? We got work to do."

CHAPTER 13
YAYO

WHEN I DECIDED to come back to Chicago after my father died four years ago, I wasn't strictly honest with my family. I was happy in Atlanta, making more money than I'd ever made before. But what I didn't know, was that the Feds had been watching me for over a year. They had so much information on my operation, they could've run that shit in my absence. Hell, they knew more than half the people on my payroll. They had wiretaps, photographs, call logs, text messages, they had it all! It was enough to lock me up until I was an old man, but being that my lawyer was a beast, he managed to get me a deal. Don't get me wrong, I was a hood nigga through and through, and the one rule of the streets is you never snitch. But I'll be real, I'm not a young man anymore, and I sure as fuck I ain't built for a long bid. I had grown too comfortable and lived a life of luxury for far too long. Plus, I had too much going on to be out of the picture, and I didn't trust my wife to hold a nigga down one bit.

I walked out of that precinct with the warning that I had three months to get them something that they could use, or I was being charged with everything they had on me, as well as interfering in a federal investigation. They wanted the plug, but I wasn't that stupid and I really didn't need those kinds of problems. The cartel had ways of finding things out and wouldn't hesitate to end my life and the lives of my entire family. I figured if I could give them a few other people, people who had already wronged me, then it wouldn't be so bad. Or so I thought. It didn't matter how many names I gave them or how many arrests they made, it was never enough. Eventually, I was running out of options, I had made a deal with the devil and there was no way out. So, I ran.

Within minutes of my plane touching down at O'Hare International, I was having second thoughts, but it was too late now. I'd had to lie to my wife and children about the reason that I decided to re-locate back to Chicago, and they were all hella unhappy about the move. The only person who even knew that I had been pulled in for questioning was my lawyer Quinn, and I couldn't speak to anyone about anything. I needed a release, but my side bitch Imani wouldn't get there until tomorrow. I know what you're thinking, but I couldn't leave her behind. She sucked my dick better than anyone I had ever known and that was saying something 'cause I knew all of the baddest bitches up and down this country. I still owned properties in the city, ones that I had before I was married. Houses that Ameena knew nothing of, so it would be nothing to have both my wife and my side piece here. Imani had just graduated law school and had been offered a job in Chicago, so she was more than happy to move when I told her the plan. Ameena was getting on my nerves more and more with each day that went by, and the way she acted towards Havana was getting out of hand. I'd warned her on more than one occasion to stop fucking with my Princess. I swear on everything I owned, that if I heard her talking out the side of neck to her one more time, I'mma fuck her up. I know what the problem was, it was that the older Havana got, the more she looked like Vee, and she's got a smart mouth on her, too. But, that's daddy's girl.

When we first came back, I had every intention of finding Vee and telling her the truth about Havana, or Heaven, as she knows her. But when I found out she had married Big H I got angrier than I had ever been before. How dare she move on, and with him of all people! I know he only got close to her to fuck with me and that in itself angered me.

I decided to fuck with her a bit and forced her to give me back the money that she took from me. Since I had to shut shit down, I was spending that bread quicker than I could make it, and I was still waiting for the will reading for my father's estate at that time.

The night Vee came and shot me, Havana was in the back of the car. She had been staying at her friend's house and they'd gotten drunk for the first time. It was really late, so I went to pick her up and she was sleeping on the backseat. Luckily, she was totally out of it. She'd even commented to me afterwards, that until she saw me the next day, she actually thought it had all been a dream. Vee sealed the fate of her and her husband with that move and, if she ever gets to know Havana now, it would be over my dead body.

I'd been lying low for the last few years. The only moves I made were power moves to help me get back what was rightfully mine. When I went to shoot up the cookout, I was aiming for Vee. That poor young girl who got hit was just a casualty of war, but I didn't care one bit.

I have tried everything to bring Big H down, but it's like he's made of Teflon. Nothing sticks to that motherfucker. He took everything that was mine all those years ago, and I want it all back, including Vee.

I never should've let her go. I should've left her with Heaven, knowing that she would be tied to me for life. Seeing how heartbroken Ameena was after finding out that the doctors had to give her an emergency hysterectomy to save her life during the birth of our youngest son, I just had to give her a daughter. She knew that she would never have any more children, and she had always dreamed of having a little girl to complete our family.

I had to leave Vee unexpectedly after the birth of my youngest son. Ameena had a real hard time and I had to be there to be a full-time dad and husband while she got over everything she had been through. I acted like I didn't know Vee was pregnant, but I had eyes and ears everywhere, so I knew the minute she did. She was so green in those days. She just didn't have what it took to be the wife of a hustler, or so I thought, until I found out about her a Big H a few years later. Anyway, I came back two weeks before she was due to give birth. I had the whole thing planned and I knew from the jump that I was leaving again, but this time I was taking what was mine.

After I decided to just admit the truth that I was married and had children, she completely overreacted about the whole thing. If she had been on board with my life plan for all of us, then things could've gone so differently. But she made it clear she wouldn't be part of the arrangement I'd suggested. I saw an entirely different side to her after that.

I was so angry at Vee, she had been down right disrespectful ever since she found out about Ameena, and I just knew that she would try to leave me. I couldn't stand the thought of one of my seeds being out there without me, so I decided it would be best for all involved if I took my daughter home to my wife. Vee just didn't understand. I had to marry Ameena, it wasn't a choice. It was all arranged by our fathers many years ago. We were promised to each other, and that's not something I could go back on. I tried explaining all of this to Valencia, but she wasn't hearing any of it. She really was one stubborn broad, and she had made her choice, and that was that. She would never be the side bitch. I knew I would never accept her having my daughter around another man. It was in Heaven's best interest to be raised with me.

If the choice were mine, the only woman I ever would've married would have been Vee, but I had to honor my father. I always knew that when my father died, I would come back here and get Vee back, and I don't care what I have to do and who I have to hurt to get her. I'm certain that I can make her see sense once Big H is out of the way.

Three months ago, the same Fed who was working my case back in the A got a transfer to the narcotics unit at CPD. It turned out he wasn't fitting in very well and he needed a bust to make himself look good to his little piggy friends. He must've got a hard-on the second he heard my name come up, 'cause he was waiting to pull me over the second my ass drove away from Imani's crib.

This time, I had an unlicensed firearm, half a pound of coke, and a twenty bags in cash on me. With my track record the coke was enough to have me sitting down for a minute. Hearing him say that they were trying to bring down Big H, it was my turn to get excited. I found out that they had successfully implanted an undercover agent in his operation, but they feared that he had gone rogue. They wanted anything they could use to bring him in.

I took that as my opportunity to get my own back and start to reclaim what was rightfully mine. They say that if you remove the head, the body will crumble. Now that he was out of the way, it was time to put phase two of my plan into action. I got my sons to hit one of their traps, but they didn't even get enough to make it worthwhile. They came out of there with less than five hundred dollars and no product. I don't know why I trusted either of them to do something right, they were both as stupid as one another. It's my fault. I spent so much time out of the house when they were growing up that they ended up just like their useless ass mother. I just couldn't stand being there with Ameena.

When I started seeing how she acted towards my princess, I just knew I had to get rid of her once and for all. I couldn't divorce her, because that would mean I had to give her half of everything I'd built, and that would be the last thing I would want to do. I just tried to make her as miserable as I could in the hopes that she would leave, and then she would walk away with nothing. She knew how our pre-nuptial agreement was set up, so she would rather stay and be miserable while still living the life of luxury, than to walk away with nothing. She's a spoiled little bitch who has been handed everything she ever wanted in her life, and never lifted a finger to get it.

CHAPTER 14
VEE

I HAD BEEN SEARCHING HIGH and low for motherfucking Yayo, but it's like he vanished off this earth. It'd been three weeks and my husband was still locked up. Time was running out and if one of us didn't find him soon, it would be too late. Once he gave his evidence, there would be nothing any of us could do.

The lawyer told me that the rest of the case had so many holes in that it could easily be picked apart. None of the evidence they had would be enough to keep him locked up, but with witness testimony, it would almost be certain that my husband would serve time and I wouldn't allow that to happen. He's always gone hard for our family to give us the life we have. Now it's my turn to do what needed to be done to hold our family together. I had to find Yayo, and I wouldn't stop until I got my man home with me.

I stopped off to grab some Chinese takeout on my way home from work. Tonight, I was going to spend the evening with my kids. It felt like forever since we'd done something simple like sat and had dinner together, but it looked like God had other plans for my evening.

I had just got back in the car after collecting our food and I thought I'd seen a ghost. It was him, just walking into the restaurant like he didn't have a care in the world. He came walking out minutes later with some takeout boxes. I waited for him to get into his car before pulling away two cars behind him. I followed him through the city, in and out of the heavy rush hour traffic. I had no idea where he was going, but he sure was in a rush.

Thirty minutes later, he pulled into the parking lot of the hospital. I was about to follow him into the building when I spotted Kymani and I know wherever he was, Harlem wasn't far behind. Being that my husband warned me not to get involved, I knew I couldn't risk them seeing me. I had to fall back, so I got back into my car and watched the entrance to the building.

I had faith that Harlem and Kymani would be able to handle things, but then I spotted Harlem's car drive out of the parking lot with Kymani in the passenger seat. I wanted to know what the fuck they were playing at and why the hell Yayo was still in the hospital.

Pulling out my phone, I phoned Harlem.

"What's good, Queen? Where you at?" he said into the phone.

"I'm ok. I'm almost back at the house. How are you boys getting on with tracing this snake, Yayo, is it?!" I said innocently.

"No luck yet, but I will let you know as soon as we find him. Did you speak to pops today?"

"Ok, erm, I have to go. I'll phone you later," I said rushing him off the phone.

Either he didn't know who he was looking for, or he was lying to me. Either way, it wasn't helping get my husband home any quicker. I would just have to sit and wait until he came out. I'd spent so long looking for him that there was no way that I was leaving now. Even if it meant I had to sit there all night.

Eventually, four hours later, he came out looking disheveled and like he had the weight of the world resting on his shoulders. It reminded me of the night that Heaven was born. I shook off the thought of my perfect daughter before I broke down and focused back on the task at hand. This man had ruined my life and taken the chance to see my baby away from me, and tonight was the night that I made him pay with his life. Yes, I was angry about my husband being locked down, but the drive behind this was Heaven. That was how I knew I would be able to take his life and not blink twice. Don't get me wrong, I'm no killer. But he killed my daughter as well as my soul, so this was his penance.

My entire pregnancy there was not a single thing wrong with me or my baby. Then, he popped his ugly ass back up two weeks before my due date, and all of a sudden, my baby was dead. It just didn't sit right with me. As the years passed, my biggest regret was not walking away and leaving the second he showed his ass up again. But also, that I didn't fight to find out what really happened. I was young, heartbroken, and alone, but I should've fought harder to find out the truth.

I drove behind him until he pulled into a diner. I watched him enter and walk straight to the table. He always sat as close to the door as he could, and always by the window. So predictable. He liked to see who was coming in and also be able to make a quick exit if he needed to. I probably should've waited to see if he was meeting someone, but I couldn't help myself. I made sure my gun was loaded, stepped out of my car, and slid my gun into the back of my jeans. But before I could close the door, I was grabbed from behind. Instantly, my instinct kicked in and I started trying to fight, but then I heard a laugh I had heard a hundred times before.

"Take it easy killa, get in the car," he whispered.

I turned around to see Harlem all dressed in black. He motioned for me to get into the car.

"Boy, are you trying to give me a fucking heart attack?" I said when we were both inside the car.

"Are you trying to get yourself killed, Valencia?" he replied in a low voice.

"Excuse me, boy? Watch who you're talking to. I'm still mama to you. You ain't that damn grown."

"Does pops know that you've got another kid? How long have you been working with this motherfucker?" he asked. His voice was low and cold.

"It's not what it looks like, baby. I know I have a lot to explain, but I owe your father an explanation before anyone. You have to believe me baby boy, I am not working with him. I just needed some answers before he dies. He's the only one who can answer me, Harlem. I have to know how she died!" I replied, now getting upset.

"How who died?"

"My daughter, Heaven."

CHAPTER 15
HARLEM

I LET that nigga make it for a few more hours off the strength of the love I felt for his daughter, but you already know what it is. The fucked-up thing about it all was that I already knew I was falling in love with Havana, but we weren't meant to be. There's no way I could be with her after I killed her daddy. She's going to hate me but I couldn't change what needed to be done. From what I knew about this cat Yayo, apart from the fact that he's snake, was that he thought he was a big name. But he was a has-been who had been living on borrowed time. His fate was sealed the second he fixed his mouth to start talking to twelve about my pops.

Mama Vee thought she was slick. I acted like I didn't see her at the hospital, 'cause I knew I couldn't say anything, as I didn't want to blow our cover and the hospital was not the place for a shootout. Luckily for me, she spotted Kymani and opted to take her ass back to her car. I knew my pops told her to sit her ass down on this, so I didn't know why she was following this man. If she knew where he was, she should've phoned me or Ky and let us handle it like we were supposed to. I didn't like to think it and I would never say it out loud, but I was starting to question mama's loyalty. 'Cause I was sure my pops didn't know about her past with this man.

Kymani sneaked by and put a tracker on ole boy's car so we could pull up and take him tonight. I was going to just straight shoot his ass but I'ma save that one for pops.

When we got to the warehouse, this bitch Ameena was tied to a chair in the middle of the room with a mail sack over her head. She was talking non-stop, it's a wonder they hadn't already shot her.

"Bruh, she has been going on and on about her husband and her sons. I'm glad you're here. I need to get out of here before I cut out her damn tongue out of her head. She doesn't stop for a breath," Santos said laughing and dapping us up before leaving.

I lit the blunt and poured me and Ky both a glass of Henny. I knew I was going to need this to be able to hear the answers to the questions I had. Something she said earlier had got me thinking and I needed answers.

"What did she ever do to you to make you want to hurt her so bad?" I asked, while taking another pull on my blunt.

"Fuck that little bitch. Ever since she came along, my life has been ruined. I am sick of watching her parade around like the Queen of Sheba. My husband acts like she can do no wrong and it grates on me. She looks just like that whore Valencia more each day and I hate her for it. I've told him plenty of times to get rid of her. I even tried to drown her in the pool more than once, but she just won't die."

"How did you end up with her?"

"That stupid husband of mine can't keep his dick in his pants and he had gotten Valencia pregnant. I couldn't have any more children and I had always wanted a girl, so he brought her home to me so I could raise her properly with her brothers. At the time I didn't care, I just wanted another baby. But the older she gets, the more she favors her mother, and it makes me sick. She is a constant reminder of the fact that I was never enough for my husband. Valencia doesn't even know she exists, she thinks she died during her birth. Many times, I have wanted to find her and get her to take her child back. But my husband warned me that if she ever finds out that Havana is Heaven, then he will know it came from me and my life will be over. He would kill me and not think twice. He is a cold man and will stop at nothing to protect that little bitch. He has always favored her over our two sons."

"What kind of sick motherfucker takes a woman's baby and lies that she died?" I asked more to myself than anyone in particular. "Don't worry, you and your husband can rot in hell together soon," I told her.

"Yo, she's awake, bruh, and ole boy just left the hospital." Ky called out from where he was sitting.

I nodded at Ky and walked outside. He came walking out after me and we got into his Benz. I pulled up the app on my phone for the tracking device that we put on Yayo's car outside the hospital and Ky started heading towards where he was. It didn't take us long to find him and when we did, we followed at a safe distance behind him.

My mind was elsewhere so I wasn't paying attention to my surroundings. All I could think about was whether this Valencia chick was really Mama Vee, and if my pops knew that she used to be involved with this motherfucker.

"Yo, ain't that Mama Vee's car up ahead?" Kymani said as she turned into the parking lot of a diner behind this motherfucker.

"Keep going and circle back. I don't want to be too obvious. Bruh, pops is not going to like this one bit."

She was so lost in her own thoughts that she didn't even see me approach her from behind. I grabbed her the second she got out of the car. I felt her tense up like she was scared, then she started trying to fight. I just laughed, and then she froze when she realized it was me.

"Take it easy killa, get in the car," I said quietly.

I had already made up my mind that I wasn't going to tell her about Havana just yet. I had to see where her mind was at first. But more than that, I had to talk to my pops. I didn't know how much he knew but he damn sure ain't gonna like this one bit.

"You can have your chance, but not tonight. He's due to give his evidence tomorrow morning, I have to get him tonight or it will be too late, and I can't risk you getting in my way. You're too emotional right now. Take yourself home and calm down. After you speak to pops tomorrow, then you can go and ask the questions that you want the answers to."

I looked into the diner and saw that he was getting up leave.

"I'm not playing Ma, go home. I got you tomorrow, I swear."

The second he walked to his car, Ky hit him over the head with the butt of his strap and bundled him into the back seat of his own car before getting in and driving away. Just as quick as that, we had him. I ran over to where Ky had left the Benz and followed him out of the parking lot.

I don't know how hard Kymani hit this motherfucker but he was knocked the fuck out. It made it much easier for us, but where was the fun in that? I wanted him to be awake so he knew exactly who did this, but that time would come. I was bored and wanted a little fun before I headed back to see Havana. I knew I should probably stay away from her but I couldn't. Someone had to tell her the truth, and neither of the parents that raised her will make it out of this alive to tell the tale.

We tied him to a chair on the opposite side of the room from his beloved wife, before slapping him a few times to try and bring him around. Eventually he woke up looking startled.

"What's up nigga? Glad you finally decided to join the party," I laughed.

"Who the fuck are you and what do you want? If it's money you're after, I can get it for you," he said, like the bitch made nigga he really was.

"Do I look like I need your money, my nigga? This ain't about no fucking money. This is about you and your loose lips. Did you ever hear the saying, *"Snitches get stitches"*? Well, you should've listened to that. My pops is locked up right now because you don't know how to keep your mouth shut."

"Listen, I don't know what you heard, but it's not what you think. I was set up. I wasn't going to go and give evidence. I've been out of town and I only came because my daughter was attacked. I'll leave again as soon as she's fit to travel, I swear."

"Come on Yayo, you've been in the game long enough to know that you don't just get to walk away from this like nothing ever happened. But I'll leave the honor of ending your pathetic life to my pops. It's awful that your daughter was attacked, why don't you ask your wife how that happened?" I laughed, although the thought of anyone hurting Havana made me feel sick to my stomach. I was still being hard on myself for not getting at that nigga before he got the chance to hurt her twice.

"I watched the cameras back, Ameena, and I've already put money on your head. You're a dead bitch walking. If I could reach you right now I would choke the shit out of you. How could you let that happen to our daughter?" he snapped.

"What's wrong, Ameena? You've gone very quiet. Why don't you tell your darling husband what you've been telling us?" I said, holding up my phone and playing the clip I had recorded of her.

"Come on, bruh, let's leave these two to catch up and get out of here so I can get to the hospital to see my girl."

CHAPTER 16
HAVANA

WHEN I WOKE up in the hospital bed I was so confused. I had no idea how I had gotten here or what had happened to me. I saw my daddy in the chair, and instantly relaxed.

"Where am I?" I asked.

As soon as he saw my eyes were open, he rushed to my side.

"Baby girl, are you ok? Tell me who did this to you?" he said.

"I don't know what happened. I was just at home, that's the last thing I remember," I replied, still searching my brain for answers. The whole thing was still so foggy, but I remembered Tip being in my house and my mother. A vision of her kissing my man came into my head and instantly I felt sick. Just my luck, I'd only ever had one dick my life and I shared it with my mother. That was just the most disgusting thing I'd ever thought.

Just then, Ashlee walked into the room with her arms full of snacks and drinks. It was like she was preparing for a slumber party. My daddy stood up quickly, grabbed his gun and aimed it directly at Ashlee, making her drop everything in her hands straight on the floor.

"Daddy! Put that down, for God's sake. We are in a hospital. It's just Ashlee."

"What is it with people pointing guns at me?! Do I have a target on my head today or something? Damn! I'm so happy that you're finally awake, sis!" Ashlee said, worsening my confusion.

"Oh, I'm sorry Ashlee. Please forgive me. What happened to her?" my dad said, helping pick the fallen snacks up off of the floor.

"Erm. I don't know exactly. She pocket dialed me, and I could hear someone hurting her. But by the time I got there, she was alone. I managed to get her to the car and I drove straight here."

"When I find the person responsible for this, I'll kill them. Where was my wife when all this was happening?" I could see that my dad was angry and his anger always ended badly for someone.

"I'm not sure, sir. I didn't see anyone when I got to the house. The door was open slightly so I just ran straight to Havana's bedroom," Ashlee answered.

"I'm going to find out who did this and make them pay. I have secret cameras set up in the house. I'm the only person who knows where they are, not even your mother knows. When I get home, I'll look at them and then I'll find the person who thought they could break into my home and do this to my baby. I'll be back in a couple of hours."

With that my dad got up, kissed my head and left the room.

I looked at Ashlee, who had taken his place at my side just as the Nurse walked back in. She checked my blood pressure, took some more blood and examined my injuries again. The pain medication she gave me was kicking my ass, and it put me back into a deep sleep.

When I woke up, it was bright outside and Ashlee was asleep in the chair right next to me. She woke up at the sound of me knocking over the pitcher of water that I was trying to grab.

"Hey sleepyhead, are you feeling any better?" she said, as she stood up to clean the mess I'd just made.

"How did you know I needed help?" I asked, ignoring her question.

"Your phone dialed Harlem's number. He could hear you arguing in the background before Tip started hitting you. He heard it all. He wouldn't take the phone away from his ear the entire time it took us to get to you. You should've seen him, Havana. He was so worried about you. There has got to more to it with you two. Anyway, Kymani and Harlem will tell you more when they get here. I don't know what they did, but they sent me straight here with you. Do you really not remember? "

"It was Tip. I remember, I just couldn't tell my daddy. I was at home, I had just finished speaking to Harlem on the phone and I went to shower. When I came out, Tip was sitting on my bed. I think my mother was somehow involved in this. He called her into the room and this old whore kissed him! I don't know what the fuck they're doing, but they're doing something. His arm was bandaged still from where I shot him the last time he put hands on me. He was so mad with me for that and he was convinced that I'd been cheating on him with Harlem. And no, to answer your question, there's not more to it. We're just friends right now. We haven't even fucked yet."

"Yet, huh? We can change that whenever you're ready, shorty."

I blushed as Harlem walked into the room holding a huge bunch of red roses. Just looking at this man made my heart melt. He was the finest man I'd ever seen in my life, it's just a shame that he had had to see me so fucked up again. He's going to think I get my ass beat for sport, now. This was the second time he's come to my rescue in less than a month.

Harlem put the flowers on the side table, which was in the

private room my daddy had insisted I be moved to. He came to the side of my bed, where Ashlee had just been standing before going to embrace her man. He reached over and moved some hair that was in my face and gently bent his head down and softly kissed my lips. Instinctively, I reached up to cup his face in my hands and deepen the kiss.

"It's good to see you awake, Havana. You had us worried for a minute there, ma. We're going to get some breakfast and leave you to talk. We'll bring you back some food seein' as you seem to have your appetite back," Kymani joked as he and Ash walked out of the room.

I moved over in the bed so Harlem could sit up beside me. He put his arm around me and rested his head on mine, which had found its place nestled into him.

"I didn't invite him there, if that's what you're thinking," I said quietly. "I think my mom is involved. She had to have let him into the house. I swear to you, I was going to end it after everything he done last time. Spending these last few weeks with you made me see how it should be, the late night conversations about nothing, the excitement each time we touch, the butterflies every time I see you, not constant arguing and interrogations every time I move. I never wanted that to end. If I had just stayed one more night then none of this would've happened."

"I know you didn't invite him there, and it would have happened whenever you left, ma. Listen, what I have to tell you is not going to be easy to hear but I will always keep it one hundred with you. I promise you that I will never let anyone hurt you again, but what I have to say is fucked up. Firstly, Ameena was fucking Tip. We caught them fucking after he did this to you. They were so wrapped up in each other that they didn't hear us even come in the house and get you out of there."

"That is so disgusting. We're mother and daughter for God's sake!"

"Well, that's the other thing. She isn't your real mom, Havana. She said your dad got someone else pregnant and he gave you to her as she couldn't have any more children. She said your dad told your real mom that you died."

"What! You can't be serious? Of course, she's my mom, Harlem."

"No baby, she's not. She told me herself. Tip can't hurt you. He can never touch you again. As for Ameena, she is being kept somewhere safe until you heal. You need answers and I'm going to make sure you get them."

"I need to speak to my daddy. Where is my phone? I need to phone him, this can't be happening right now."

I didn't want to believe what Harlem was telling me, but a part of me had always felt disconnected from my mom. She had a great relationship with the boys, she showered them with love and affection, but she was never like that with me. I needed to speak to my dad and find out the truth, but deep down, I think I always knew something was different.

CHAPTER 17
BIG H

WALKING out of that courthouse today was the best feeling in the world and I couldn't wait to get home and spend some much-needed time with my family. Even down to last night they hadn't found Yayo, so I was certain he would be there today and fuck my life up. When I woke up this morning, I saw a text message on the burner phone that I had and knew today would be a good day.

My case was eventually thrown out due to a lack of evidence against me. It cost me a lot of money and I had to call in a few favors, but the judge who was trying my case had to recuse herself. Apparently, someone leaked some pictures of her in a bar with the prosecution. It was all a set-up, of course, but it made the local papers, so she had no other option but to step down. Then, there was the case of the star witness having not turned up to give his evidence. The new judge had no choice but to let me walk. I think the hundred grand that was deposited into his account this morning may have helped. None of that mattered now, I was free as a bird and I couldn't wait to get home.

I told Vee that it would be hours before I got processed to leave, so she could go and prepare for my homecoming feast.

I was starving hungry and I couldn't wait to tuck into one of my wife's home cooked meals. I said she could send Harlem down here to pick me up. Really, I wanted the time to speak to my son in private before we got home. I had to go through some shit with my lawyer Imani before I could leave.

When I walked outside, my son was sitting on the hood of his Benz waiting for me. His eyes were glued to his phone so he didn't see me until I was right in front of him. We dapped it up and I hugged him before getting in the car.

"How it feel to be a free man again, Pops?"

"Boy, walking on the dirty sidewalk ain't ever felt so good. I can't wait to get home. I'm hungry than a motherfucker, but first you need to get me up to speed on what's been happening?"

We spent the next thirty minutes discussing the businesses. Both the legal and the not-so-legal businesses we ran were very profitable, and all ran smoothly in my absence. I'd had to let them open up shop again when I realized I wasn't going to be out straight away. All of my workers were warned to be extra vigilant.

Listening to my son talking, I couldn't help but feel like there was something he was keeping from me. I know I wasn't around until he was fifteen, but in the last six years we had grown so close. It's almost like I'd always been in his life. Being that we are close, I knew that there was something that he wasn't telling me. I would leave it alone tonight, but in the morning, I would question him more on it.

When we got back to the house, Vee had done her damn thing in the kitchen as usual, and I couldn't wait to get started on eating it.

"Where are my kids? I expected them to both be here."

"I wanted us to talk in private first. Harlem baby, you can make a plate to go, but you need to leave me and your daddy to talk."

I watched as my son made two plates of food with his greedy ass.

"You know I can't resist Mama's cooking. Pops, hit me up in the morning, we got business to handle. Have a good night, y'all," he said as he kissed his mama and left out the door.

I watched my wife suspiciously as she busied herself preparing my plate of food. She put it down on the table in front of where I was seated, and placed a glass next to it. She then walked over to the bar area and grabbed the entire bottle of Henny and some ice, she poured us both a drink before taking a seat opposite me. I watched as she shifted uneasily in her chair, fidgeting with her hands, something she always did when she was nervous.

"Well?" I asked after sitting in silence for a few minutes.

"You know I love you, right?" she started.

"Mmm Hmm," I replied, between bites of chicken.

"Ok, so there is something I never told you, something I had kept buried and never spoke about. So you know I told you about my ex? Well, what I didn't tell you is that it's Yayo," she spat his name out with such bitterness.

"Ok. Why didn't you tell me?" I asked.

"I wanted to bury my time with him deep down and never bring it up again. He almost destroyed me. When I left him, I changed everything. I stopped being Valencia and started going by the name Vee. Valencia was nothing but bad memories and heartache," she cried as she said the words. "I had a daughter and she died. I'm certain it was because he stressed me out so much during my pregnancy. But by the time I came around from the drugs that he had insisted that I have, he had cremated her. When I got discharged, he left town 'on business'. I took that as my chance to leave. I packed everything I owned and took the first flight to New York. Six months later I met you and you changed my life. I am so sorry I didn't tell you before. Please forgive me."

"I knew about Yayo, Vee. But how could you not tell me about the baby? Even when you became pregnant with Brooklyn, you still didn't tell me. How you could you keep something like that from me?" I stood up, grabbed my phone and keys, and then I walked out of the house before I said something I couldn't take back.

I had to get out of the house and away from my wife before I really hurt her feelings. I always knew she didn't like talking about her ex, and knowing Yayo, I just figured that he had broken her heart. But a baby isn't something I ever thought she could keep from me. I just couldn't look at her right now.

Pulling out my phone, I called Harlem.

"Where are you? I need some weed and a drink before we go and deal with this bit of business we have to sort out."

"I'm just at the hospital visiting someone, but no worries, Pops. I'll meet you at the crib. I'll be about thirty minutes. You know the code to get in the front door."

"Bet," I said. Ending the call, I turned the volume up and tried to clear the thoughts running through my mind. The way I was feeling, I would fuck around and kill this mother-fucker Yayo before I found out anything that I needed to know.

CHAPTER 18
HARLEM

I HATED to be the one to break it to Havana, but I had to keep it real with her. In the short space of time that I'd known her, we'd got really close and she deserved to know the truth about Ameena. I wish I could've told her the truth about everything, but I couldn't just yet. I would when the time was right.

Havana was getting sleepy and my pops sounded like he needed me, so I made my excuses and kissed Havana once more before leaving the hospital. I promised her that I would be back to see her tomorrow.

The entire drive home, I was trying to figure out what to say to my pops. How could I tell him I was falling in love with Havana now that I knew she was Yayo's daughter? And how could I ever be with her if I was involved in her father's death? My head was all over the damn place, and although I had only known her a short time, I never thought I would feel this kind of love again.

By the time I reached the crib, almost an hour later, my pops was drunk and high as hell. I'd never seen him in this kind of state, so I knew that whatever Mama Vee told him must've been bad. I hoped my thoughts were wrong but I knew from what I'd managed to piece together that she was Havana's mom.

"What up, Pops."

"I needed to get out of the house so I could process the bomb Vee just dropped on me. I just knew if I stayed there it would've turned into an argument, so I left."

"What did she say?" I asked before I dropped another bomb.

"She was in a relationship with Yayo before we met. Between me and you, I knew that already but 'cause I didn't fuck with him no more I didn't care that she was with him before. Honestly at first, I did it just to get under his skin. But then I fell in love with her. When I mentioned his name in the visiting room that day, I'd expected her to tell me the truth, but she didn't. She also kept the fact that they had a baby together that died. I just don't understand why she kept all of that from me. I was honest about everything with her from the jump."

"I caught ma following him. I think she was going to try to kill him. I grabbed her outside a diner and made her go home, that was the night me and Ky got him."

"How do you know that she wasn't just meeting him? I don't know what to believe with her right now, but I don't trust her one bit."

"I'm certain of it. She broke down in the car and told me she couldn't tell me anything until she spoke to you. The thing is, I don't think her daughter is really dead. I've met someone Pops, and I think I love her. But then I found out that Yayo is her dad," I went on to tell my dad the story of what happened the night I killed Tip.

"You said you love this girl, huh?"

"I think so, Pops. It's just something about her. But with everything going on, she's probably gonna run a mile when she finds out the truth."

"You know I've got no option where Yayo is concerned,

don't you? If I let him go now, he'll forever be a threat to us. Especially after Vee finds out about Havana. He's been keeping her a secret all these years, so when the truth comes out, he won't react well."

"I know, but Havana can never find out that we were involved." I hated to lie and I knew secrets always had a way of coming out, but that's a risk I was willing to take for her.

"Let's go pay this motherfucker a visit. I've got questions that need answering."

I got up and walked out of the crib behind my pops. The way this crazy motherfucker was walking, there ain't no way I was getting in a car with him behind the wheel.

"Yo, we'll take my car. You don't need no DUI on the same day you got free again," I laughed.

CHAPTER 19
VEE

I KNEW that when I told my husband the truth he would get mad, and I knew that I was risking everything, but I had to come clean. I should've been honest with him from the start, so I had nobody to blame for this situation but myself.

When he walked out on me, I knew I had two options. I could either sit here crying or I could get out there and take control. I decided on the latter, so I went to get changed. Five minutes later, I was walking out of the house dressed in a fully black Gucci tracksuit with matching sneakers. I had tied my hair into a messy bun and added some bright red lipstick to set the look off nicely.

I got into my car and turned the volume up high as I sang along to my playlist. I loved these tunes so much, they were like my anthems. I listened to nothing but R&B and I especially loved the late 80's to early 90's era of music. There was nothing you could be going through that there wasn't a song that was sang about the same problem. So many of these songs had meaning to me, and despite the fact I listened to a lot of these same songs while I was carrying Heaven, I had a lot of good memories to a lot of them, too.

When I pulled up at the warehouse, I was ready for action.

I was pleased to see only one car in the lot, so I knew there would only be one or two of the lower ranking members of the organization guarding the place.

I mentally prepared myself for what I was about to do. Something which I should have done a lot of years ago. I'm going to kill Yayo and from me, he would definitely deserve what was coming to him. This man destroyed my soul and Karma had come to collect.

I was swinging my hips as I walked in the door. I had to look like I was in control at all times. I was the wife of a boss and it was time I acted like one, instead of a scared little bitch. But that went out of the window when I walked in and saw a woman tied to a chair on the opposite side of the room from Yayo.

"Who the fuck is this bitch?" I snapped at the worker who was there, I forget his name.

"Erm, I'm not sure. I just know Harlem said I had to keep them both alive until Boss Man gets here. I've tried ringing him, but I'm just getting his voicemail," he said nervously.

I walked over to Yayo and stared at him for a minute, but before I could speak, he started.

"Valencia baby, untie me and we can talk properly."

"I am not your baby. Anything between us died the day you killed my baby girl. She was fine until you showed your ugly ass face," I snapped back. "You killed a part of me that day and I have never been the same. This is nothing less than you deserve. I should've done this a long time ago."

I walked to the cupboard we had in the room and picked my weapon of choice. Firstly, I pulled out the blowtorch. I had every intention of burning this motherfucker like he burnt me. Turning the blowtorch on, I walked toward him.

"Come on now Valencia, think about what you're doing," he said.

"You bitch! You ruined my life!" the woman spat.

"Bitch, I don't even know who the fuck you are, nor do I

care. This is between me and him."

"He's my husband! And you are the whore that ruined my life. Anything between you involves me!"

"Haha! Haha! Haha," I fake laughed when she said that.

"Do I look like I give a fuck about your life? You chose your life when you married this piece of shit. I care about my life, and getting revenge for what this motherfucker did to me! Now, I suggest you shut the fuck up and let me do what the fuck I came here to do before I think it's a good idea to turn this beast on you and burn your ass to pieces seein' as you want to be so involved," I shouted back. I knew I had to stay calm and not let this motherfucker get under my skin. What I really didn't understand was why his fucking wife was here, too.

I held the blowtorch out in front of me, turning up the flame as high as it would go, I stepped closer to Yayo. I held the flame onto his chest. The smell of hair being singed instantly hit my nose but it was the smell of burning skin that really made me feel sick. I knew I wasn't cut out for this torture shit, but I had to keep my game face on so nobody knew of the internal battle I was having with myself.

All I could hear was his screams as the burning intensified. Moving the flame up and down his body, even onto his legs until he could take no more, he finally let out words that really fucked my mind up.

"Please Valencia. Stop!! She's not dead! Heaven's not dead!"

"I don't believe you. You would say anything. But there's nothing you can say that will change your fate. You sealed that when you spoke to the police about my husband. You know, I used to think the sun shined out of your ass. But really, you're nothing but a sad, pathetic, weak little man."

"He's telling the truth. She's alive," his wife shouted from the other side of the room. "He made me raise her as my own, but I hate the little bitch. She looks just like you."

I don't know what came over me, but I'd officially had enough of the bullshit. I pulled my nine out of the waist of my jeans and shot her in the leg. She was screaming and crying but I didn't give two fucks.

"Bitch, didn't I tell you to shut the fuck up!?" I screamed.

I walked back over to Yayo and pressed my gun into the middle of his forehead.

"Do you mean to tell me that you faked our child's death and left me grieving for nineteen fucking years? What kind of sick twisted motherfucker…"

I got so angry I couldn't even get my words out. I lowered my aim and hit him in the shoulder. I tried to regain my composure before I continued.

"What kind of person does that? What did I ever do to you, Yayo? I was a good woman to you. I did everything I could to make you happy. It is you who went off and got married, not me! You never should've come back! You should've stayed with her and let me and my Heaven be!"

"Who are you kidding? You never understood. You know exactly what it was, ma. I told you a hundred times, I didn't choose to get married. I came back to you; I would've always come back to you. All you had to do was play your role and we all could've been happy. But no, you wanted it all. You would've taken her the minute my back was turned. This is your fault as much as it's mine. You made me take her! I was going to tell you when I came back, but you acted like you were so much better than me. You made me so mad. You know something else? When I shot your son's girlfriend at the park that day, I was aiming for you and when you came and shot me outside my house that night it was Havana, well Heaven, in the back of the car. The first memory of her mom is seeing her shoot her dad!"

I couldn't listen to anything else. I raised my gun again and closed my eyes. Before I could pull the trigger I heard a shot. I opened my eyes and almost pissed on myself to see my husband and son standing there. Lil' Harlem was holding the gun and looking real fucking mad. My husband stood behind him staring at me like he wanted to jump over here and kill my ass. Yayo was still screaming from the shot Harlem just fired into his chest.

"What does he mean, Ma? It was him who killed Mya and you knew all along? You let this nigga walk the streets knowing what the fuck he did? You comforted me knowing that you caused her death? Are you fucking serious right now? Is that what it is, Ma?"

"Harlem baby, just listen to me." I rushed toward my son, but he pushed past me.

"She knew. She came to my house and shot me, but she didn't have the heart to finish the job," he laughed.

"Shut the fuck up, Yayo. I wish I did kill your ass. I should've shot you the day you came back and I was eight months pregnant," I spat, and then I turned to look to my husband and my son. "I can explain everything. Please, can we just go home and talk about this," I was pleading, but it was falling on deaf ears.

"Vee, get the fuck out of here before I really do something I'll regret. Take your ass home and check on my damn kids. I'll speak to you when I get there and not a minute before," my husband's voice drowned out every other sound in the room, and the tone of his voice let me know that he wasn't playing, either. It wasn't often that my husband raised his voice. But when he did, he commanded respect, and everyone knew exactly what time it was.

There was nothing else I could do tonight, so I walked out and made my way home, trying to process what the fuck had just happened. If what Yayo said was true then I had a daughter to find and years of missed time to make up for. I didn't know how my husband was going to take the fact I'd lied to him but all I cared about was finding my baby and bringing her home to her family.

CHAPTER 20
HARLEM

HEARING that Mama Vee knew this motherfucking Yayo was the one who shot Mya made my blood boil. I didn't know what the fuck to do right now, but it took everything in me not to shoot her in the ass when she walked past me. You had these moments in life where everything changed in the blink of an eye, and this was one of them for sure. Nothing could ever be the same again after this.

I was going to kill this motherfucker, but now I was really going to torture his ass. He was going to pay for his sins tonight. I hoped he was ready to meet his maker, because if there was one thing I was sure of it was that he wasn't leaving here alive. Running up on him, I hit him so hard the chair almost fell backwards. I was raining blows all over this motherfucker wherever I could land them and showing no mercy.

"You killed her? She had her whole life to live for and you shot her like she was nothing," I was shouting and punching him again and again with each word.

"I'm sorry. I never meant for it to happen like that. I have felt that guilt every single day, she wasn't much older than my daughter. I've got too many bodies to count but this is the only one I ever lost sleep over," he managed to spit out, the blood now starting to come out of his mouth.

"Son, go sit down, pour a drink, and smoke something because you need to calm down. This one is yours, though," my pops slapped me on the shoulder and I went to sit down next to my two workers.

I pulled out a pre-rolled blunt from my pocket and put fire to the tip. Santiago and DJ had heard everything and could both see the look on my face. Both of them had known Mya and they also knew how fucked up I was after her death. For us to finally be in the same room with the man who murdered her was something we all had waited a long time for. DJ came and handed me the bottle of Henny he was drinking and I took it to the head. I needed to get high to calm my nerves, so I smoked the rest of the blunt and pulled my phone out to shoot Kymani a message. I looked back over to where my pops was standing in front of Yayo.

"We were friends, Antonio. I never expected this from you. We came up in these streets together, son. Why would you turn like that? The Antonio I know would rather be dead than snitch on one of his own. But from what I've heard, you've been snitching on everyone for a long time. Isn't that right? I've been hearing lots of things about you. I was going to come here tonight and give you the opportunity to right your wrongs. But then, not only do I find out about this history you have with my wife, but I find out you are the man responsible for my son's pain. How you could shoot that poor girl? She had everything in front of her and you took that away from her to try and get back at Vee? You took her baby and said she was dead, but you still wanted to get revenge. Make that make sense!"

"You wouldn't understand. Everything you ever touched turned to gold and I was sick of it. I got into a situation that I couldn't get out of, and it was me or them. So, I chose me. Vee didn't deserve what I did to her, but she's shown that she could never have been trusted. Just look at the secrets she kept from you. I won't beg for my life, but I will ask just one thing from you. Let me just speak to my daughter and tell her I love her one last time," he spat the first part with so much jealousy it made me sick. A man should never envy what another man had, he should get out there in the trenches and get it for himself.

"You're not going to ask me to spare your wife?" Pops replied calmly.

"Na, fuck her. I watched the cameras back from the house so I know what she did. She deserves everything she gets. It's lucky you already disposed of that motherfucker Tip. After what they did to my baby girl, they would've both been dead anyway."

I decided to step in and say something.

"Listen up, old man, you don't ever need to worry about Havana again. I got her, but she does deserve an explanation. I'm going to hold the phone and let you speak to her but let me get a few things straight first. If you tell her what's happening here, then I will shoot you in the head and not think twice. And you need to tell her the truth about her mom. She deserves the whole truth about Vee and why you did what you did. She needs it to help her heal, but don't worry, I'll be the one to heal her heart."

I grabbed his phone from the side where I'd left it when we first brought him in, and saw thirty missed calls from Princess and a few more from a number that wasn't saved. The Princess contact had a picture of him and Havana smiling at the camera. I pressed call and put the speaker on the phone so everyone could hear.

"Daddy, I've been calling and calling, I need to ask you something."

"Princess, I've gotten myself into a situation and I am going to have to go away for a long time until things die down. But I want you to know that I love you more than I have ever loved another person in my entire life. You know the code to the safe in my office. Take everything. It's all yours."

"Where are you going? I want to go, too. Ameena told me that she is not my real mom. Is it true?" she asked, I could tell that she was trying not to cry.

"Yes baby, it is. I'm sorry and I wish I would've told you the truth but I just couldn't. I'm a selfish man and I'm ashamed of my actions. Your grandfather made me marry Ameena. It was arranged between our fathers when we were small children. I did what I had to do, but I never loved her. I kept her and the boys in Atlanta where our families were but I lived here, and that is how I met your mom. Her and Ameena knew nothing of each other. When your grandfather found out of my relationship with your mother, he said he would cut me out of everything if I didn't stop seeing her and go back to my wife 'cause I was embarrassing the family name. For eight months, I went back and played the role but knowing that your mom was pregnant and alone I went back to her before you were born. She was so angry when she found out that I was married, I just knew that she would leave and take you with her and I couldn't let that happen. I did something I have been ashamed of ever since, but I did it for you. It was all so I could keep you with me. I told your mom that you died during your birth. There have been so many times that I wanted to admit the truth to you and to her, but I couldn't bring myself to do it. I'm sorry Havana, my Heaven. I hope one day you will forgive me. I love you." I cut the phone off before she got to ask any more questions.

"Don't you worry, I got her from here. I'mma be the one she calls daddy from now on." I gave him a wink and walked toward my pops.

"You done?" he asked.

"Yea, let's get this shit done so we can go talk to Ma."

"I'm not dealing with her right now. I might just fuck around and kill her ass, too," he laughed.

Both of us turned and fired our guns, killing both Yayo and his bitch ass wife Ameena.

"Yo DJ, call the clean-up crew. I'm out," I called over to my boy.

Walking outside in the morning sun, we both took a deep breath. I think we both knew that nothing would be the same in our family after this.

"I'm starving,. Let's go get some breakfast and work out the next move." My pops said.

"You always thinking about your stomach. We done just killed two motherfuckers and all your greedy ass can think about is breakfast?" I replied while shaking my head, opening the door and getting into the car

CHAPTER 21
BIG H

I COULDN'T BELIEVE the shit that had happened in the last twenty-four hours, and at this stage I really didn't know if I could forgive my wife. We had been together eighteen whole years and she'd kept this from me that entire time. I always thought we had such a great relationship because we were always honest with each other, and even after all this time, we were still so in love. We had the kind of relationship people envied, that real hood love that nothing and nobody could ever come between. We were supposed to be best friends, and outside of my children, she's my everything. I just didn't know if I could ever look at her in the same light again.

Don't get me wrong, I was happy that her daughter was alive, but I also knew that had I known about her, I would've gone to the ends of the earth to get answers for Vee about what really happened. And I knew that we would've found out the truth a long time ago. It was her own sneaky ass fault that she lost more years with Heaven than she needed to. My reach was far and wide, and I would've found that girl and raised her at home with the rest of our kids. Because of Vee's lies, Mya was dead and my son was left brokenhearted. All of this could've been avoided, and that's why I was so angry.

"What next, Pops?" Harlem asked from across the table.

"I really don't know, son. Your mama has been blowing up my phone, but I'm just not ready to hear her right now."

"I'll take you back to my crib. You can chill there while you figure out your next move. I need to go chop it up with Kymani and go check in on Havana."

I knew my son was in love with this girl just by the way his eyes smiled when he mentioned her name. The same way I used to smile about Vee. And if this girl was anything like her mama, I knew that he had found the one. I just hope she's not like her snake ass father, 'cause she would end up back with him sooner than later.

We got in the car and headed back to Harlem's crib. I needed to take a long hot shower and smoke a blunt to help me figure out how I was going to handle this shit with my wife.

After handling my hygiene and putting fire to my blunt, I laid back on the guest bed and turned the TV on. Within minutes, my ass was knocked out and I didn't wake up until I heard a noise downstairs. I picked up my phone to check the time, and it was almost nine o'clock. I couldn't believe that I had slept the entire day away.

I got up, brushed my teeth with one of the new toothbrushes that Harlem kept under the sink in the bathroom, and headed downstairs to see what all the noise was about.

Walking down to the basement, I saw that my whole of my crew was here. Harlem had a dice table and a domino table set out. The bar was fully stocked and there were two beautiful women to serve the drinks. He even had a stage and pole set up to one side, so I knew that this was going to be a wild night.

"What the hell you got going on down here?" I asked.

"I started to wonder if you were dead up there. You slept

the whole damn day. We didn't think you would be in the mood to go out, so we thought we would bring the party to you. For real Pops, everyone wanted to see you and we'd arranged a little homecoming party for you. But after everything that happened, I knew you wouldn't want to go out and you would for sure need a drink. Go and enjoy yourself, you deserve it. I've got to pop out, but I'll be back in a couple of hours. I've got a bit of business to deal with."

Harlem and Kymani walked out, leaving me with my crew. These were all the older heads, my day one niggas. Most of us had been friends since grade school and few real ones that we picked up along the way. My son was right, though. This was just what I needed.

"Let's get these drinks poured and throw these dice. I need to make back some money and you know I'mma be taking everything you got!" I said with a laugh. They all laughed back because they knew I always got lucky with the dice.

After drinking a few glasses of rum and smoking a few blunts, I was really starting to ease up and enjoy myself. After everything that had happened, I needed to get fucked up, and that was just what I intended to do. I cut my phone off and paid attention to the pretty woman who was serving the drinks. She had the biggest booty I'd seen in a long time. Turning around, she noticed me eyeing her ass and winked at me before putting an extra switch in her step. I had to remind myself that I was still a married man, no matter how angry I was with my wife right now. I'd fucked one other woman since I made shit official with Vee. I'd got the odd bit of head here and there, but never fucked them broads.

That shit all changed recently when my lawyer went off sick with COVID right before my trial and sent in his replacement. A cute lil' caramel chick with a big booty named Imani. She was short, curvy, and thick in all the right places. She made it clear from the first meeting that she wanted me. I told her I was married, but she didn't care. On her second visit, she didn't wear any panties under her skirt and kept crossing and uncrossing her legs, showing me her freshly waxed pussy. It was all over when she dipped her finger in her soaking wet pussy and licked it after telling me she had been dreaming about my dick print.

My boy was harder than a motherfucker and I needed to bust a nut. My plan was to just let her suck it, but she had me ready to shoot my seeds down her throat within minutes. Shawty did mad tricks with her mouth. She really blew my mind and my dick. While I was trying to regain my composure, she hiked up her skirt, and sat on my dick. Her pussy was just as good as her mouth, and shawty could ride that dick like she was in a rodeo. After that, she'd been arranging meetings every other day, and each time, we would discuss the case and then fuck.

Part of me hated myself for being unfaithful, but the other part of me loved the excitement of it all. The feeling when I was fucking her in that room, knowing there were guards just outside and that someone could walk in at any minute, was so exciting and had me feeling like a young man again. She made it clear when I fucked her in the back of her Range Rover after court that she didn't want this thing with us to end, and if I was honest, neither did I. But I needed to worry about getting shit straight on the Homefront first.

CHAPTER 22
HAVANA

AFTER HARLEM LEFT the hospital yesterday, I was so confused. But this time, it wasn't the concussion clouding my thoughts, it was the reality that my entire life was based on a lie. I must've tried to phone my daddy a hundred times, but kept getting his voicemail, and Ameena wasn't answering, either. Someone had to tell me what the fuck was going on before I completely lost my shit. Everything Harlem said had been playing over and over in my mind. I thought back on my life, and the only thing that stuck out to me, was the fact that my mother was always more distant with me. I always thought she loved my brothers more than me, but daddy always said it was because I had always been a daddy's girl and that she was jealous of how close we were.

We always had a nanny to take care of us, so I never really spent that much time with my mother. Ameena was never really what you would call a 'hands-on' parent. She would only really spend time with us when my father was around, or if we were in front of people. She would put on a show of being the perfect wife and mother. Growing up, I never really understood why my dad stayed with her. They never really got along and argued with each other whenever they were in the same room for more than five minutes. This was just how they were and had been for as long as I could remember.

When I got a little older, I found out that my daddy had other women in his life. I would hear him on the phone and he even used to take me to meet them at their houses. I knew not to say anything about them to my mother. These were women who made him smile, not like when he was with my mother. I secretly used to hope he would leave Ameena and one of them could be my new mom. They were always so nice and attentive. Now I knew they were just trying too hard to impress him.

One day I asked him why they stayed together if they weren't happy. His only answer was that life was easier that way. I knew in that moment that I never wanted to have a relationship like they did. I would never be the type of person to settle for less than I deserved. As I sat here with my whole body aching from yet another beating at the hands of my so-called boyfriend, I wondered how that girl had gotten so lost and ended up in a relationship with someone like Tip. Someone who thought it was ok to beat my ass over and over again. Someone so controlling. It made me sick to think of him fucking me and then going and fucking her. Mother and daughter, well supposedly, but he didn't know that! I wish I could bring him back to life and kill his ass all over again. I hated that I had given him so much of my time.

Right about now, I didn't trust anyone but Ashlee and Harlem. He's kept it one hundred with me from the start and I liked that. He had already shown his loyalty and that meant more than anyone would even understand. The nurse said I should be able to go home tomorrow after Dr. Grayson came to see me. The thing is that I didn't know where *home* was anymore.

I didn't have any of my things with me, so I couldn't just get a taxi to a hotel like I had originally planned until I realized that I didn't even have any money with me. I was going to have to ask Ashlee to take me back to grab some clothes and get my bank card, at least. I was mentally planning what I needed to get from the house and where everything was, so I would be able to get everything and get out of there as quickly as possible.

The sound of my phone ringing snapped me out of my thoughts. Looking at the screen, it was a picture of me and my daddy. I quickly answered the call. I listened as the man I had loved and held on a pedestal my entire life admitted that everything I knew to be real was a lie. A lie created for his own selfish reasons. Hearing the words coming from him, I knew that everything that Harlem told me was true.

The phone was disconnected before I got the chance to ask him anything else. I didn't even know my real mom's name or where to even start to try and find her. I must've cried myself to sleep, because I woke up to Harlem moving hair out of my face and kissing me on my head. I opened my eyes and look at him before moving over in the bed so he could lay next to me.

"I spoke to my daddy. He told me the truth. Everything you said was true. Not that I thought you were lying, but I thought you had wrong information. Oh, I don't know! I'm so confused. I don't know what to do. My whole life is a mess and the one person I trusted has let me down more than anything I ever could've imagined. If I can't trust my own parents, I can't trust anybody. Now I can't get through to my dad and he said he has to go away, so I don't know when I will see him, but I don't even know my real mom's name. How can I find her if I have nothing to go off of?"

"I've got someone trying to find out more for you so we can start looking for your biological mom. If you're sure that's what you want. It's time to start living for you and stop being daddy's little girl now. You're gonna have to get on your grown woman shit. Don't be too trusting, but also realize that not everyone you meet is going to lie to you, baby girl. Real recognize real, remember that," he said in a serious voice, before smiling again.

"I know I do. It's time I stood on my own two feet. I've decided that I'm moving out of the house. It's something I've wanted to do for a while now, but my father would never allow it. I don't know where and I don't have the first idea about how to go about buying a house. But I have money, so I guess I'll have to get some help. I don't even want to go back to my house after everything that happened there, but I need to get my stuff. I just hope I don't see Ameena, I might shoot her just like I shot her boyfriend Tip."

"You don't have to worry about that. Ashlee has been there all day packing your shit up and the movers will be going to collect it in the morning. I would've helped do it myself, but I figured you would prefer Ash to do it, in case you had anything private in there. As for Ameena, let's just say that you won't be seeing her any time soon. I have a feeling that she went to find Tip. I want you to stop worrying about all of that. Everything will be ok. You just have to give it time. I'm going to be back in the morning when you're discharged and I'm taking you somewhere," he said and kissed my head again.

Something about this man just made me feel safe. If I was only sure of one thing right now, it was that I wanted to get to know him more and see where this thing with us could go.

CHAPTER 23
VEE

AFTER THE WAY my husband spoke to me earlier, I just knew to bring my ass straight home. There hadn't been many times in our marriage that he'd shouted at me like he did tonight. He was usually so placid and calm. I had never seen him as angry as he was today. I knew I'd fucked up, but damn. He could've at least given a bitch the chance to explain. I hated how hot-headed he was sometimes, when he was like that, he didn't listen to rhyme nor reason. There was no point in talking to him at all, 'cause it literally went in one ear and out of the other.

I'd cleaned the entire house and changed all of the beds to try and keep busy while waiting for him to come home, but he still hadn't shown his face. For the last few hours, I have been trawling the internet trying to find any trace of my daughter, but I was getting nowhere. I thought all teenagers had social media profiles these days, but I couldn't find her anywhere.

I knew I was going to have to hire a private investigator to help me find her. I could only hope and pray that she wanted to have a relationship with me. I didn't know how I was going to explain this shit to my kids, but I hoped that they understood and didn't react the same way H did. I didn't want this to tear my family apart.

I gave up hope waiting for my husband at around 2a.m., by then I figured that he wasn't coming back any time soon. Brooklyn was out with his girlfriend and Liberty had her best friend staying over, so they'd been in her bedroom all night. Luckily, neither of them saw just how upset I was. I'd already drank two bottles of wine before I went looking for some weed. Opening my husband's drawer, I found a bag containing some pre-rolled blunts, which was lucky for me because there was no way I would be able to roll one as drunk as my ass was right now.

I was just about to close the drawer when something caught my eye. It was notification lighting up the screen of the burner phone that my husband had been using while he was in jail. I picked it up and unlocked the screen. When I went into the text messages and read the contents, my heart dropped. I couldn't believe the shit I was reading. I took the blunt and lit the tip, inhaling the hay. With each message I read, it became more and more clear to me that my husband had been fucking this woman.

He had the nerve to talk to me about lying and he'd been fucking the damn lawyer we had been paying to get his ass out of jail. There was text message after text message from this woman telling my husband how much she had enjoyed their meeting and that she was hungry to taste his dick again. One even went as far as to say that he fucked her better than anyone she'd ever been with. That was it for me, I got so angry that I threw the glass I was drinking from at the wall and started smashing up the entire room.

In all of the years that I had been with him, this was something I'd never had to deal with before. I always knew that there wasn't a bitch in these streets that could come between me and my man, or so I thought! He knew of my past and the fact that I had been cheated on previously, when I was unknowingly the side bitch to Yayo's wife. He also knew without a doubt that cheating was something I would not tolerate. The evidence was all there so he couldn't deny it, no doubt he would try, though. I was so hurt, but the anger was bubbling in my stomach like a volcano that was about to erupt. I didn't care that he was in his feelings about Heaven, he was definitely going to have to see me about this. Grabbing my car key, I put my Gucci slides on my feet and left out of the house. I knew he could only be at Harlem's, and I had every intention of letting him blow off steam, but playtime was over.

When I pulled up outside my son's house, I was shocked to see so many cars parked up outside. It looked like there was a party up in here and I was about to crash it. I left my car in the driveway and walked to the door. I put the code in the keypad and walked straight into the house. Looking around, I couldn't see anyone, which meant they had to be down in the basement. The second I opened the door, the smell of weed and sound of laughter piqued my senses. Without thinking twice I walked down the stairs, but once I had the room in view, I wished I had stayed my ass at home. It was niggas and hoes everywhere. I couldn't believe this motherfucking Harlem was having a party with strippers and all kinds of shit going on.

As soon as my husband noticed me, he pushed the girl off of his lap and stood up. "Vee, what are you doing here? This isn't what it looks like."

"Na nigga, you carry on. You look like you was having a good ole feel of her thot ass. This is exactly what it looks like, just like these text messages from Imani are just what they look like. I can't believe that you fucked that bitch! How could you do that to me? To us? You can keep your lying ass right here. I don't even want to hear anything you gotta say."

"Don't come in here trying to embarrass yourself, Valencia. I told your ass I would come back when I was good and ready. You're in no position to say anything. You know I how I get down, so don't keep playing with me, coming in here showing your ass in front of all these damn people. Why don't you tell them all what a lying, two-faced snake you really are? Go on, Vee, seein' as you want to tell them something. Why don't you tell them that you have been lying for our entire relationship about a baby that you had with ya boy Yayo?" he spat angrily at me.

He was drunk as hell, because no matter what, he would never lose his cool in front of so many people. If he was in his right mind, there is no way that he would think it was ok to disrespect me so openly.

"Fuck you, Harlem! Nigga, you must be drunk or high to think you can talk to me like that! You are outta your goddamn mind. You done played with the wrong one!" I screamed as I turned to walk out. Rushing up the stairs, I almost bumped straight into my son.

"Ma, what's going on?" he asked. "I was going to come by and see you in the morning. I've got some shit I wanna talk to you about," he said

"I ain't got shit to say to anyone right now. Move out of my way." Pushing past Harlem, I opened the door and made my exit.

Picking up the planter that I got Harlem when he moved in, I chunked it at my husband's car, smashing his window in the process. The alarm on his car was going off and drawing too much attention, so I hopped in my car and left.

CHAPTER 24
HAVANA

DR. GRAYSON CAME to see me first thing this morning and told me that she was happy to discharge me this afternoon as long as I had someone to look after me. She let me know that she would be back later with my prescription, and then I would be able to leave.

The second she left I pulled out my phone so I could place a call to Harlem.

"Hey baby girl, is you good?" he answered, sounding like I had just woken him from his sleep.

"Were you asleep? I'm sorry, I know it's early."

"We had a get together for my pops, so shit got a bit wild. But it's all good," he replied.

"Well, Dr. Grayson said I would be able to leave today. I'm healing and should be back to myself in no time," I said, but the line was quiet for a moment.

"That's good news, baby. Let me get up and have a shower, then I'll come scoop you up."

I said goodbye to Harlem and phoned Ashlee.

"Girl, you have got too many clothes for just one person to live in this room!" she said into the phone as soon as she answered, letting me know that she was still packing up my stuff from the house.

"Are my brothers back yet?" I asked.

"No, it's just me here," she replied.

"I need you to go into my daddy's office and open the safe. Put everything in there in a bag, but keep it with you."

"Girl, I am *not* about to rob your daddy. His cartel looking ass will come and shoot me."

"Ashlee please, he told me to empty the safe. If you go in the office and move the picture of me that's on the wall, the safe is behind it. The combination is my birthday backwards."

"Ok, but I'm telling you now, if your daddy comes to me about this, I'm snitching like a bitch. That man is a scary motherfucker."

I couldn't help but laugh at her stupid ass. She was always so dramatic, but there was nobody that I trusted more.

"Holy shit, Havana! I'm gonna need a suitcase to empty this thing!"

"Girl, don't be so dramatic. There can't be that much in there. He never keeps too much money in the house."

"Ok girl. You'll see what I mean soon enough."

I chatted with Ashlee a while longer before Harlem walked in. I said goodbye to my friend and turned my attention back to Harlem. When I say this man was the finest specimen I had ever seen, it's not a lie. He was the most gorgeous man I'd ever laid eyes on, and from the moment we met, he was all I had been able to think about. He was just so confident, almost in a cocky way, and he exuded power. Whenever he was around me, my heart beat faster, my palms sweated, and my pussy quivered. She was down there jumping around now like she was all excited, and she hadn't even met him yet.

Harlem walked straight over to me and kissed me before he spoke.

"So, where's this Dr.? What did you say her name was again?" he asked.

"Dr. Grayson and she should be here soon," I replied.

We settled into conversation, with Harlem telling me about the party they had last night, and how he had organized a trip for us this weekend. He let me know that the movers were bringing my stuff over and it would be stored in the garage until I was well enough to go through it all.

"I don't know what I did to deserve you in my life, but I'm grateful for you and everything you've done for me. I can't wait to show you just how much once I'm healed again," I said with a smile, letting him know that I wanted him.

Before he got the chance to answer me, Dr. Grayson walked into the room and Harlem looked like he'd seen a ghost.

CHAPTER 25
HARLEM

AFTER MAMA VEE crashed the party night, Pops really turnt up. I had never seen him as drunk and high as he was when I left them niggas in the basement at 5a.m. I gotta give it to these old heads, they could all still hang like they were young. Shit, even me and Ky tapped out before half of them, and we are savages.

Only a couple of hours after I crashed out, I woke up, irritated by the sound of my ringing phone. Answering the phone to Havana's sweet voice made me forget that. Just the sound of her voice made me happy. I almost forgot that she was coming home today, until she mentioned it. Hearing her say her Doctor's name was Grayson, I was hit with a wave of nauseating grief. It came at you like that when you lost someone you loved, no matter how many years passed or how much you thought you had healed.

Grayson was Mya's surname and when she got accepted into Harvard to study to become a doctor, I got her a Rolex with the words *I love you Dr. Grayson* engraved on the back. I was so proud of her and the fact that she was following her dreams. She believed in me more than anyone, and when I was failing school because I was too busy with this gang shit, it was Mya who helped me study for exams and graduate school. She knew that I had dreams outside of these streets and we had a whole future planned out before that mother-fucker Yayo killed her.

Even knowing that it was his fault that the love of my life was dead, I still don't want to stay away from Havana. I never thought I would fall in love again, but I had and I couldn't blame her for the sins of her father.

I got myself ready to go and get my girl, but being that my pops and some of his friends were still drinking in my base-ment, I figured I would just take her to a hotel until they left. I wasn't quite ready to tell her about Mama Vee yet. I just wanted a few days of peace with her before it all kicked off again.

Walking into the hospital, I was happy as hell knowing that everything was finally put to rest. We had got rid of Yayo. Tip was gone. Pops was home and business could finally get back to normal. All that was left now was to tell Mama and Havana about each other, and we could start to move forward.

I was helping Havana pack up her stuff so she was ready to leave, when the doctor walked in. The instant I saw her, it was like the air had been sucked out of my body. My knees went so weak, I had to take a seat. It was literally like looking at a ghost, and she didn't even look at me twice. She continued telling Havana what she needed to before turning to walk out of the room.

"Mya?" I said, but she kept walking.

I followed her out of the room. Havana was calling after me but I didn't stop.

"Mya," I called out again, but the doctor kept walking. I caught up to her, and grabbed her by the elbow, turning her to face me. "Mya, I know you hear me talking to you. Don't act like you don't see me."

"I'm sorry, but my name is not Mya, so I didn't know you were speaking to me. You must have me confused with someone else. Now, you need to let go of my arm before I call for security."

I let her arm go and she walked away. Pulling out my phone, I sent a text to Kymani.

Bruh, I need you to get down to the hospital now. I saw Mya, she is alive. I typed and pressed send before I felt Havana walk up behind me.

"Is everything ok?" she asked with a concerned look on her face and clearly still in a lot of pain. I grabbed her bag off her before answering.

"She just looked a lot like someone I used to know. Don't worry, let's go." I pulled her into my side and wrapped my arm around her shoulders.

As we walked out of the elevator and into the parking lot, my mind was all over the place. I didn't care what that woman said, she was Mya. I would recognize those eyes anywhere. I'd spent enough time lost in them. I was running everything through my brain about the night that Mya died so much, that I didn't even see the man in the ski mask walking towards me until it was too late. He pulled out his Glock and aimed it at me.

I saw the flash of light before I felt the bullet tear into my skin. I tried to reach for my piece but the next one hit me, then the next one, and the next, before I fell to the ground. Instantly, a pool of blood was beginning to form around me. Havana was screaming for someone to help us. I could hear people rushing around me, but I couldn't keep my eyes from fluttering closed.

"Harlem, come on, stay with me," I could hear the nurse saying as they were trying to move me.

I could still hear Havana crying and I was trying to speak to her, but the words were not coming out. I could feel that there were people rushing around me, asking questions. I could hear machines beeping and Havana crying. Suddenly, everything went black.

… To be continued.

CONTEST RULES

THIS RELEASE WILL HAVE 1 CONTEST. THE CONTEST IS
REVIEW AND SCREENSHOT YOUR PURCHASE TO
contestsgrandpenz@gmail.com BY 1/17/22 TO WIN
1ST- $50 CASHAPP
2ND- $25 CASHAPP
3RD- $15 CASHAPP

WANT TO BE A PART OF THE GRAND PENZ FAMILY?

To submit your manuscript to Grand Penz Publications,
please send the first three chapters and synopsis to
grandpenzpublications@gmail.com

Made in the USA
Monee, IL
14 June 2022

97990393R00079